BIRTHRIGHT

Birthright

a novel
by

VAASANTHI

Translated from the original Tamil by
VASANTHA SURYA

zubaan
AN ASSOCIATE OF
KALI FOR WOMEN

Birthright first published in English in 2004 by

Zubaan
an associate of Kali for Women
K-92, 1st Floor
Hauz Khas Enclave
NEW DELHI - 110 016

ISBN 81-86706-62-8

Cover design: Shruti Sanganeria

Printed at Raj Press, R 3 Inderpuri, New Delhi, 110012

Birthright

Translator's Introduction

What is the value of a female life?

In most parts of India, the cult of the mother-goddess flourishes even today, exalting life, fertility and abundance as attributes of the female. Yet women themselves are sometimes constrained to acquiesce in, and to aid and abet the devaluation of their own sex. Surely this behaviour runs counter to basic human impulses, and to the instinct for survival. How did this come about ?

It is this phenomenon of female self-inflicted pain and hatred which is the theme of Vaasanthi's insightful novella, and the unanswerable force of its central plea for gender justice and equality is what drove me to translate it.

Kadaisee Varai (*Birthright*) lies squarely within the tradition of the modern Tamil novel, which has, for close on two centuries, been a vehicle of social change, grappling with the gender issues at the core of the modernizing process. A perception of deep-seated discrimination and injustice has troubled several women writers, but what makes Vaasanthi's writings distinctive is her delving into the complex psyche of the educated, privileged, and apparently 'liberated' woman in Tamil Nadu. She reveals with remarkable dispassion that a personal struggle for empowerment, and the claiming of a hitherto denied space, can often be at the expense of other, less fortunate, women. Armed with a sense of victimhood and misplaced pity, an elite woman can always find, within the culture and the tradition, sympathy and even sanction for attitudes and actions which actually demean and destroy the lives of other women. In this case, the 'liberated' woman is a gynaecologist. Interestingly, the most respected and sought-after profession for women in India today is medicine. Especially in gynaecology and obstetrics, women have an assured place, with the 'lady doctor' being almost worshipped as an awe-inspiring symbol of science and technology. How this new 'deity' melds into and moulds the traditional 'mother goddess' Mangamma is the fascinating area of individual choice explored in this novel. What takes place is the transformation of woman from object to subject, from one who is acted upon, as much by internal compulsions as by external circumstances, to one who consciously goes beyond them.

Among humans the biological imperative of procreation takes intricate social and cultural forms. In pre-modern, agrarian communities. it is held to be every man's and every woman's duty to produce progeny. Childlessness is perceived as a singular misfortune. The Sanskrit word for "hell" is *put.* By carrying on the line, a son (*putr*) or daughter (*putri*) are believed to save a person from the hell inhabited by those who have left no descendants. It is one's *putr* and *putri* who open up the way to the abode of the ancestors. However, under fully developed patriarchy, the *putri* came to occupy a lower ritual and social status than the *putr*. A woman's status as a daughter was eclipsed by her role as a wife and a mother in her marital home, which was where she was said to really "belong". The daughter's obligation to care for her parents, and to perform their obsequies seems to have vanished, even as she lost the right to regard her parental home as her own, and to inherit her father's property. For, needless to say, the performance of the death rituals confers not only blessedness but also tangible worldly benefit. Today in most parts of India, it is only a *putr* who is thought to save one from *put*, as though his very maleness qualifies him to light the parents' funeral pyres and thus unite them with their ancestors. Unwritten codes proscribe women from certain actions connected with the procedure of disposal of the dead, and these injunctions have been rationalized and justified as being based on a consideration of the so-called 'delicate' nature of women. This notion that a girl simply cannot do what is necessary for her parents at the time of death seems to be at the root of the preference for sons found throughout patriarchal India. This results in many subtle and gross forms of discrimination against daughters, and against women in general. It is not surprising that these attitudes often come to fruition in women's low self-esteem. Within that sour fruit can sometimes be found the bitter seed of self-destruction: female infanticide.

Thanks to modern medicine, female infanticide has been reincarnated as female foeticide: a "safe" option, performed by doctors who are encouraged to abort children in the interest of population control. (Amniocentesis or sex-determination tests, used in China, also a patriarchal, modernizing society, are illegal in India. Instead, to get around the law against sex-selective abortions, usually one doctor does a 'scan' ostensibly to do a pre-natal check and if a female foetus is revealed, another doctor performs an abortion — a legal procedure permissible as a population control measure.)

The modernizing process, far from eliminating patriarchy, has often reinforced it because it has been so uneven. Existing inequalities of class, caste, and community have deepened and, with the spread of consumerist life-styles they have strengthened ingrained gender biases. For instance, the custom of demanding dowry in the form of jewellery worth several gold sovereigns has become ubiquitous among the subaltern sections, and even among the very poor. Holding ostentatious wedding celebrations for one's daughter has become a matter not just of prestige, but of honour, and the "custom" has become so widespread that many people now go into lifelong debt on that account. A daughter then continues to be a "fire in the belly". When patriarchal conditions prevail, and one has become convinced of the need to limit one's family, one chooses to have a son, rather than a daughter. Ironically, then, the modern idea of family planning has made it possible for people to exercise an age-old preference.

Women are significantly outnumbered by males in almost all parts of India. A study by Sheela Rani Chunkath and V.B. Athreya, quoting figures from the Census of India, shows that the number of females relative to males has been decreasing over the past fifty years. (*Economic and Political Weekly*, April 26, 1997) In 1951 in Salem District the ratio was 1016 females for every 1000 males – which reflects world population figures, showing the better survival rate of human females, all other factors being equal. But by the time this novel came to be written, in the 90s, there were only 849 females to 1000 males. Chunkath and Athreya's paper examines gender specific mortality rates taken from PHCs (government primary health centres): in 1995 neo-natal mortality rates for Tamil Nadu state were 44.3 per thousand for girl babies as against 36.9 for boys, and for Salem 85.4 per thousand as against 43.7 for boys. The figures for Dharmapuri are 100.1 as against 45, and Madurai 70 as against 39.7.

There are unmistakable indications that these figures reflect discrimination of many kinds, including the practice of eliminating females at and before birth, which has been confirmed by many investigations. Cases of female infanticide – the official euphemism: 'death due to social causes'— began to be unearthed by the press in Madurai in 1986 (*India Today*). By the early 1990s it became clear that the practice had been common in Salem and Dharmapuri as well. As a literacy activist, I met and spoke with some of these mothers and fathers in 1992 in a Salem village. These daily wage labourers told me that a girl meant much more expense and trouble from the very beginning than a boy.

Sometimes they appeared strangely flippant, basing their preference on seemingly trivial considerations, and sometimes they sounded callous, and mercenary:

"As soon as her hair grows, we have to buy clips and ribbons! Then ear-rings, and bangles. A girl has got to be given jewellery and ornaments." And: "When she goes to work, she fetches less wages." But probing a little deeper, I found deep-seated anxieties: "A boy can go anywhere, be with anybody. But a girl is 'fire in the belly'. We are nervous about her until we marry her off." And: "Without a grand wedding and a dowry, she will have no respect in her in-laws house. So we have to get into debt and can't come out."

Arrests of guilty parents and mothers-in-law began to take place. The Government of Tamil Nadu announced an ambitious 'cradle-baby' scheme, pleading with all those who did not want their girl babies, to deposit them in cradles placed in primary health centres, promising to accommodate them in orphanages or place them in foster homes. The cradles remained largely empty. Rather than leave them in the care of strangers, and feeling incapable of bringing them properly in an openly misogynist society, the mothers of girl babies preferred to kill them as soon as they were born. Or even before they were born. A woman doctor showed me a hospital ledger recording the sudden death of little girls a few days after they were born and taken home. She explained to me the traditional methods of poisoning, starving, smothering, and choking by which female infants were eliminated by their own grandmothers. With the advent of pre-natal scans, and the widespread practice of abortion as a method of population control, female foeticide has become the preferred option for those who are determined not to have girl children. This doctor was at pains to deny that she was one of those who do scans to weed out girls.

In Vaasanthi's novel, the protagonist is a woman doctor who

does exactly that. She candidly admits to her friend, the sociologist, that she scans and aborts female foetuses on demand, claiming that she does it out of 'compassion'. We see how, coming from a society in which being female seems to mean being just a little less than fully human, not only a desperate mother or an embittered mother-in-law, but even a medical practitioner can be driven to give vent to a subliminal sense of injury.

As Mano tells her story, a persuasive argument emerges for enlightened fatherhood, which alone can set right the skewed relationship between the sexes. In keeping with Vaasanthi's perceived commitment to eschew literary fashions and to write in the popular idiom, her Tamil is eloquently simple. Her characters emerge naturally from a recognizable landscape where even myth and mystery have a scent and colour as familiar as the turmeric and vermilion-anointed god-pictures in the puja room. But there are no concessions to romanticism. It is not without pain that Mano finally pulls out of her psyche the dagger-like contradiction between life-affirming and life-denying facets of the culture into which she has been born. The ageless, shapeless stone called 'Mangamma' yields to Mano's shaping. A livable future emerges, the woman doctor is healed of her inner fury, and truly becomes a healer.

Being dynamic, popular religion and culture need not preserve stereotypes of oppression, or remain steeped in obscurantism and superstition. Symbol, ritual and icon can all work as aids to self-actualization: this is an understanding which already exists in the culture and acts a kind of antidote to literalism and dogmatism. They can sometimes be effective psychological tools for resistance and liberation. Interestingly, as Chunkath and Athreya point out in the article mentioned above, the People's Science Movement has used these as well as other features of contemporary folk culture in the technique of *kalai – payanam* (roving street theatre). In the late nineties the Tamil Nadu Science Forum conducted an intensive campaign of social mobilization, staging scores of lively skits and plays on the theme of gender justice in villages and towns. Hundreds of enthusiastic young men and women took part. Soon afterwards, Dharmapuri district's primary health centres actually recorded a modest decline in female infant mortality rates, as well as the number of female infant deaths. This is a sensitive and imaginative effort to address the problem of attitudinal change, which is the theme of Vaasanthi's novella.

VASANTHA SURYA

One

I waited for him to answer.

It seemed as though the words I had just spoken hadn't entered his consciousness, or that he hadn't grasped their meaning. Or perhaps it was because he had, that he remained silent. I understood the quandary he was in.

The beach was almost deserted by now. The descending darkness had spread out over the sea and far beyond. In the stealthily pouncing beam of light from the distant lighthouse, the foaming edges of the waves became visible only when the water spiralled and came tumbling back to dash against the shore. A wave drenched me to my knees and drew back, hollowing the sand out from under my toes.

I was sliding very slowly, over the edge of the universe. Was this what it felt like when the earth gave away at Sita's words: Enough! Enough, O Mother who bore me! Now take me unto yourself! Hollowing and widening, the breach would have opened a passage leading downwards, and Sita would have stepped into an underground chamber. And when it was all over, a howl would have risen up fit to shake the earth: 'SITA, SITA!' The television *Ramayana* came to mind. Rama, all made up and costumed, and howling away.

'Shall we go?' said Shiva, 'you have to catch the Cheran don't you?'

'Yes,' I said, turning at once. Holding my chappals in one hand and not bothering to shake off the wet sand clinging to my feet, I walked on. I didn't ask him: 'Why haven't you answered my question? ' It was he who spoke.

'This condition you're laying down— it's very strange, Manohari,' he said in an accusing tone. 'No man would accept it.' I felt neither regret nor surprise at his answer. What I did feel was a burning irritation.

'*You* don't accept it. Leave it at that.'

'You've got to understand why !' he said heatedly. 'No self respecting man—'

'No, Shiva. Don't say anything more. No need now for an argument about who's got to understand whom.'

It worried me that my emotions might get out of hand. A gust of wind loosened my hair and blew it over my face, its strands poking me like needles. It was too dark to see his face clearly. Yet, when I turned sideways to push my hair out of the way, and glanced in his direction, I could see his bewilderment.

'You think there is no need to discuss this?' It was clear from his voice that his emotions were getting out of hand.

'None,' I said, holding my ground.

'So the chapter is closed?'

'Yes.'

He walked on, a tight expression on his face. In the circle of light around the Gandhi statue were five or six cars with their rich young owners lolling against them. The coconut-water man had decided it was time to shut shop and he was busy putting things away in his cart.

'Let's have some *elani*, Shiva,' I said, feeling suddenly quite cheerful. My mind felt as if it had grown lighter. I wasn't about to probe the reasons.

'All right,' Shiva said, still with that tight look on his face. I was the one to run to the cart and say, 'two elanis' and I was the one who counted out the money. The youths lounging against their cars and yakking away looked us over for a few moments, and then returned, bored, to their yakking.

Shiva gulped down his elani and said abruptly, 'Shall we get going?' as though he had suddenly run out of patience.

'I'm ready,' I said. I walked with him to his motorbike and seated myself behind him.

The street lights were very bright. On the gigantic poster of Jayalalitha that stood at the street corner, right under her broad smile, were the words: WE SHALL GIVE EQUAL RIGHTS TO WOMEN. Like the gracious blessing of the Paramacharya himself. Shiva's enthusiasm of an hour ago had vanished. Poor fellow, I thought. I felt slightly guilty and yet from the feeling of relief that I had at that moment, I understood that there was no point in trying to change his mind.

'How you people complicate life!' he said, turning slightly in my direction.

Cold, the breeze, as I asked him, 'Whom do you mean by "people"?'

'I mean those of you who talk feminism.'

I broke into a laugh. 'I don't think there is any 'ism' or 'isnotism' in any of this!'

'Don't make a joke of it. This is a serious matter.'

'You're the one who made the joke, Shiva, not I. Okay, let's drop the subject.'

He didn't talk after that. When he dropped me off at the railway station, as we'd planned earlier, I saw that he was hesitating and I said, 'You don't have to come inside, Shiva.'

'Are you sure?' he said, being very formal and correct.

'Quite sure,' I said, smiling and holding out my hand. 'We're both still friends.'

But he seemed unsure of that as he caught hold of my hand.

'Don't misunderstand what I say... but if you don't give up this obstinacy of yours, you're just going to end up all alone.'

'Don't pronounce a curse on me,' I told him, still smiling. Then I freed my hand and turned sharply around to walk into the station. But his words pursued me, and when I found my compartment and sat down, they jabbed at me like thorns. 'Ada, go 'ya! So what if I'm alone!' I muttered.

The passenger sitting across from me said, 'What?'

I switched off the light as though I hadn't heard him and lay down on my berth. When the train reached Salem it felt as though I had re-entered a safety zone. Maanikkam, our driver, was standing there, waiting right at the spot where my carriage came to a stop, having calculated exactly where it was going to be. He took my bag.

'Are you doing well, Akka?' he asked, as though I had just got back from a long trip abroad! Yet, just two days earlier it was he who had seen me off at the very same station. He went on: 'After all, how can the air or the water or the food in the city be anything like what we have here in our own place, Akka!' Somehow the affection and pride that resonated in his voice always filled me with energy.

'Is Appa doing all right?' I asked him.

'He's fine. Got up at three thirty and chased me off to the station!'

I smiled and leaned back in the seat. It felt as though the lush green on either side of the road and the coolness of the air were seeping into my veins and muscles, relaxing both mind and body. What Maanikkam said was quite right. No heaven anywhere could match this.

Appa was waiting on the verandah. The glow on his face at the sight of me felt like a warm embrace. What Shiva said came into my mind — something about how no man with any self respect would. . .

'. . . how was the seminar, Amma ?' Appa was asking.

'Oh, the usual thing. How are you? Is the blood pressure okay?'

'It's behaving itself,' said Appa, smiling. 'Raasamma swears she hasn't been anywhere near the salt container.' Raasamma, the girl who did our cooking, stood smiling deferentially at a respectful distance, near the door.

'Come 'kka,' she said, 'Shall I get you some coffee?'

'Yes, please. I'll go and wash my face,' I said, and went to the bathroom.

I am Big Sister to practically everybody here, except old Muniappan, the gardener. These people have been with us for two or three generations. To the entire third generation I am 'Akka', and when they call me that I feel the burden of all those generations pressing down upon me. I fantasize that my very security is bound up in that closeness. More than their need for me is my need for them. I don't know if Shiva would feel any of this. Quite likely, he'd make fun of my "capitalist mindset". Or feel shocked by it.

Washed and refreshed, I went to the dining table. Along with the coffee, Raasamma brought a newspaper and placed it before me. That was what was always done for Appa, and ever since I opened my clinic and set up practice, it's done for me too.

'You are also working, no? As much as any man? For that you should get proper respect or not?' said Raasamma one day.

'Is it only after seeing how I compare with a man that you'll give me respect Raasamma?' I teased.

When she laughed and said, 'That is the usual custom, 'kka!' I had to shut up.

When I had finished, Raasamma set my tiffin on the table and announced, 'Meenatchi phoned twice while you were in the bath 'kka. She wanted to know when you'll be going to the clinic. There's some urgent case, it seems.'

'In that case, I'd better get there. Just give me some more coffee Raasamma.'

'Ayye, then I made a mistake in telling you. Eat just two idlies before you go, 'kka.'

'Send them to me later. If it wasn't urgent, Meenatchi wouldn't have phoned.' I downed the coffee in a single gulp and hurried to the clinic adjoining the house.

'You've come, Akka!' said Meenatchi, with obvious relief. 'Two cases arrived this morning from Belukurichchi. One is a septic abortion. The other is a second delivery. Both are kicking and howling! I couldn't budge, couldn't move an arm and a leg even.'

Without answering, I quickly went through the case sheets as I hurried to have a look at the patients. Meenatchi looked thoroughly exasperated and at her wit's end. 'This whole business of women giving birth — there should be a law against it, Akka!' she had once protested to me. And yet, every time a baby was born in the nursing home, it was Meenatchi who went into an ecstasy as though she had been witness to the greatest miracle on earth.

Once inside the clinic, and in my white gown and gloves, it felt as though I had been transformed into a different person. Escaping from one prison cell to land in another — like spirits jumping between body-cages, as the proverb goes.

This Meenatchi and Paavaayee, too, who does the sweeping and cleaning in the clinic, both have extraordinary faith in the world of spirits. Paavaayee says a hundred years ago, right here on this land, a woman climbed onto her husband's pyre. Her soul, she says, still haunts the place.

'If she turned herself into a burning stick for his sake, doesn't she belong in heaven? Why should her spirit wander about here?' I demanded.

But Paavaayee took my teasing question seriously. 'Poor thing, she must have some unsatisfied desire or other'

They've even given it a name — Mangamma. On new moon and full moon night Paavaayee and Meenatchi smear turmeric and vermilion on a rock they've set up in the garden, and make offerings of milk. They don't know it, but I think that spirit's got hold of me as well. I feel some kind of force inside me that's beyond the human.

The two Belukurichchi cases were screaming away, just as Meenatchi had said. Twenty years old, the abortion case must have been, not more. Luckily it wasn't as critical as I'd expected, although she was half dead with fright. I started treatment at once. Her husband had died a year ago, apparently. When she regained consciousness, I told her quietly, 'Look here, next time don't go to any old medicine woman. Come to me, I'll get rid of it.' The girl gave me a dumbfounded look, then broke into tears.

The delivery case was quite simple, no complications. No need to howl like that just for labour pains. Something else was making her howl. This was the second — the first was a girl. What was this one going to be? That was what the screaming was about. Meenatchi said the husband and the mother-in-law were waiting outside. When she screamed *Ayyo*! *Amma*! what she was really doing was trying to see if the wellsprings of compassion would open up for her.

'This woman must get a boy somehow. That Mangamma Thayee must open her eyes and take one look at her,' muttered Paavaayee.

The woman's shrieks of 'Daktaramma, save me Thayee!' gave me a trance-like feeling that I'd become Mangamma herself. As the infant came out screaming shrilly all of us stood around in a terror of suspense.

'A boy!' announced Meenatchi.

The woman who'd just given birth to it stared in disbelief, then clutched at my hand and kissed it as though she'd gone crazy. 'Thayee! You're a goddess, Thayee!' she gasped and began to sob.

Wearily I detached myself from the rejoicing taking place around me and went to wash my hands. The very sight of that frenzy and those happy tears was humiliating. The husband and mother-in-law were passing around lumps of sugar. I wanted to tear them to pieces that very instant.

'It's enough now, please do the operation,' the husband said to me, in a large-hearted way. Meaning, No need for her to be in this business any more, she's performed to our satisfaction, she can retire!

Little by little, the sounds of the nursing home subsided. As I prepared to leave for home, with a sense of having done my bit for that day, it arrived. *That case*.

The girl looked terror-stricken. A little conversation calmed her down a bit. Name? Ranjitham. Age: Around thirty. How many deliveries so far? This'll be the sixth. How many survived? Three. All female. Not asking her what had happened to the other two, I examined her anaemic eyes. Which month is it now?

'It's the sixth, 'nga.' Suddenly she seized my hands and held on tight.

'Daktaramma! Only you can save me!' The fear I saw in her eyes was something I was quite used to seeing, and yet every time it set off a powerful tremor, as it was now doing.

'What can I do? ' I muttered. 'Can't abort it now. If you didn't want children why didn't you go in for an operation?'

Her grip tightened and began to actually hurt. I was amazed: where did all that strength come from inside that bag of bones? There were no tears in her eyes, only dry sobs welling up from the underbelly.

'They want a son, an heir. What can I do? They say you can find out before birth. By looking inside. Look inside Thayee, and tell me! If it's a female, get rid of it Thayee!'

Silent, I stared at her. A real bag of bones. Then I said, softly, 'It's a crime, according to the law, Ranjitham.'

'I'll never breathe a word of it outside, Thayee. Save me! Or I'll just have to take poison myself. I can't - Thayee - I just can't have it if it's a girl.'

I stroked her back lightly. Meenatchi came at the sound of the bell.

'Looks like there is a problem with the foetus. Get ready to do a scan,' I told her.

It could be seen clearly on the scan. The 'problem'. A clearly developed female foetus. I didn't say a word to Meenatchi but just got on with the job. Tonight or early tomorrow Ranjitham would go into labour. A healthy female child would be born. Dead.

Why did you do such a thing ?

Meenatchi wouldn't ask me such a question.

Two

Every once in a while I have a peculiar sensation of being connected to all the women who come to my clinic, by bonds that extend beyond this birth. Embracing their concerns is like recruiting an army, all by myself, for my own cause. When my classmate from college, Kamalini, who's a professor in Delhi, came here the first time, she was a bit startled by the cool dexterity with which I handle such cases. 'Is it really you, Mano, doing such things ? Under the law, it's a crime, Mano.'

I remember how I was pressing down on the abdomen of a patient with one hand at the time. My eyes were on the scan screen and her words didn't really register. I was watching the infant in the womb whirling around, swimming happily there on the screen. It did a somersault, legs apart and buttocks up, showing its little trident of female genitalia quite clearly. The computer was telling us that January 30th was its due date, and here the foetus was, leaping about with the exultant throb of life, utterly unaware of my watching it. Cocksure of itself in its safe fortress, it stuck out its tongue and sucked at something. Kamalini was gaping at the screen, entranced.

'Do you still have the heart to do it, after you've seen this ?' she said softly, in an awed voice. Smiling a little, my eyes still on the screen, I told her, 'You wouldn't understand how merciful a creature I really am.'

'Merciful, my foot!' Kamalini retorted, disgusted.

I wasn't prepared to get into an argument with her. Every

argument is useless, utterly futile. Arguing about this thing with a person who doesn't have the slightest idea what it is to breathe the air of these parts is especially meaningless.

Yet I was glad to help Kamalini out in any way I could. She wanted to talk to women working in the fields, she said. She wanted to get their songs on tape, she said. She was doing research on folk songs, she said. So we decided to go to the villages around to meet women in their homes.

When we drove out of the clinic grounds and left the town behind us, Kamalini heaved a sigh of relief.

'*Appa* ! Now I can breathe. I was practically choking in that clinic!'

I laughed but didn't answer.

'Why do you have to live in this village, Mano? At least you could live in Salem. You did so well at college. If you had stayed on in the city, who knows where you would have got to by now.'

The only answer I could make to that was another laugh.

'If I didn't happen to live here, what would have happened to your research?' I asked flippantly. She looked uncomprehendingly at me.

'Tell me why you stay here,' she said again.

I hesitated, flinching. It felt like being asked to reveal an intimate secret. To display it in the open for all to see. 'This is where I have to be, Kamalini,' I managed to say, haltingly. 'I don't want to... just take off and go anywhere else.'

For a while Kamalini remained silent. Then she said, 'Is it because you are your father's only child?'

'Not just that. There are so many other considerations,' I said, careful not to get entangled in specifics. I added hurriedly, 'Of course that *is* an important reason – that I don't want to leave my father.

'Are you never going to get married ?'

'Of course, I'll get married! If there's a man who will consent to come and live here!'

'There's no man who will do that,' said Kamalini with finality.

'Why not? Is it only a woman who must go off to her husband's house and no answering back, is that it? Why can't a husband go to his wife's house?'

Kamalini laughed. 'Who'll come and park himself here in this village? Only some fatso, some useless loafer, who has his eye on your property – some such fellow may turn up, if that's what you want.'

'So, if nobody's willing to come, so be it. I'll just remain the way I am.'

Kamalini didn't say anything. To her, the whole thing must have sounded like a dialogue from a Tamil film. *Daughter sacrifices wedded happiness for sake of aged father*! What an unnecessary sacrifice, she must have thought, derisively. I had no desire to explain anything to her, or to anybody.

'Hasn't there been anyone at all... whom you've felt close to so far?' she said at last, curiosity and concern jostling together in her voice.

I stuck out my underlip in denial. Shiva's face bobbed up on a wave of memory. Hurriedly, I pushed it down. Fortunately, Kamalini didn't probe further.

The car came to a stop on a road that ran into a low-lying area lined with huts. Immediately a crowd swarmed around us, instantly recognizing me and welcoming me with shouts of 'Akka-come! Akka-come!' Kamalini was quite amazed.

'This Akka has come all the way from Delhi to listen to you sing your songs. She is going to record them and take them with her. So please sing !' I said. 'Your songs will be heard in the big city of Delhi.'

'Ayye... what songs do we know?' the women said, deprecatingly.

'Sing! I'll pay you money,' said Kamalini, very businesslike. There was a short silence.

'*Oppaari* is the only thing we know to sing. And three-quarters of that we've forgotten,' said an old woman.

'Then just sing that, please,' said Kamalini, turning on her tape recorder. The women stood about in little clusters. The old woman ponderously lowered herself onto a grinding stone as if it were a stool. A kind of silence fell and strangely quelled the cheerful bustle of a few minutes earlier. I was still contemplating the sheer weight of it when her voice rang out, deep and firm, in the dirge she had chosen to sing:

O silver fire-box!
O packet of beedies!
So prized by that Bheema
Who entered my life
And then went and died
Like a spent firecracker
In that prostitute's lap
He gambled and stumbled
Lost his way in strange streets
O he never got home!
That love potion the whore brewed
How can you enjoy it
At your own funeral feast?

The old woman's voice was a keening moan. In the enveloping silence I felt I had become a woman whose man lay sprawled in a whore's house as though fate had led him there. There's the corpse – they've brought it to the street corner. Like a crazy woman I'm waiting here for him, with his silver matchbox and a pack of his favourite beedies. Cheated. Betrayed.

In the holy town
Where I was born
The sugar's so fine

And yet, mother mine
O woman who bore me
No sweets have you sent me

And yet mother mine
I know that you love me
You're not like the other
Who tells tales about me
My golden one's mother

O woman who bore me
If I told you my woe
Your bright golden face
Would lose all its glow.

With a sob, the old woman stopped singing. Tears stood in the eyes of the women standing around. One was wiping her eyes with the end of her sari. Were they really stirred by the meaning, or was it that eerie, stomach-churning wail that melted them where they stood? It wasn't clear which it was, but from the tears that were brimming in my eyes it was evident that there was something that bound everyone in that circle together, and that I was also one of those ensnared. Kamalini was hurriedly scribbling something down in her notebook. Glancing at me, she remarked in English 'very interesting!' Would this blurring, this softening and coming together that had taken place among these women at this point in time be recorded in her research findings? Doubting it, I got up.

After a couple of days Kamalini went off to Madurai district to record more dirges sung by women there. She must have been driven away by her mixed feelings about me.

There was a light knock at the door and when it opened slightly, Meenatchi's face appeared in the gap.

'The woman who had the operation after delivery says she wants to go. She wants to see you 'kka.'

'At this time? It's midday!'

'The husband's arranged for a "pleshar-car", he's so pleased at the birth of a son. The mother-in-law's come too.'

'Okay, let her go. Have they cleared their bills etc.?'

'All done, 'nga.'

'Okay, send her and her husband to me. Not the mother-in-law.'

The girl was still weak. The husband came along, careful not to touch her, "unclean" from the blood of childbirth as she was.

'Thank you very much, 'nga!' he said with great cordiality. 'I'm taking her home, 'nga.' The girl sat there, head bowed.

'If a girl had been born, you'd have sent her to her parents!'

'Nothing like that, 'nga!' he protested. His face oozed foolishness. 'It's all the same to me 'nga!'

'If you take her with you, you'll have to be careful. She has had an operation, do you understand?'

'Oh, we'll be careful about all THAT, 'nga.'

'If you're not careful, it'll be dangerous for the child,' I said, insistently.

'All right, 'nga.'

Meenatchi came to call him for some reason and he took leave of me with another *vanakkam*. At once, the girl grabbed my hand and began to cry. 'You spoke the truth, 'nga, it's only because it's a son that there's all this kindness. If this one too had been a girl, they'd have sent me away forever. They had it all arranged beforehand.'

'Arranged what?'

'A second marriage – they had even chosen the girl.'

'Even before the child was born?'

'Yes, Amma, that's what I am telling you, 'nga! Seems the parrot astrologer said only a girl would be born.'

The girl gave a grin. I felt a lurching in the pit of my stomach. I had a feeling of *déjà vu* – as though I had met this woman before.

'If it had turned out to be true, what could I have done, 'nga? I had made up my mind too. If something like that happened, I would have tied my two girls around my belly, and climbed down into the well.'

'*Chee, chee*, why should you die?'

'There isn't any other way, 'nga,' she said huskily, with a constricted throat. 'You wouldn't understand. You're people with means.'

When the husband came to fetch her, she trailed after him like a lamb. To the waiting taxi – the 'pleshar-car'.

There were no more cases, Meenatchi said. At last, I thought, and got up. The clinic was utterly quiet and subdued. Ranjitham, the woman who had delivered a still-born female child yesterday, had left in the morning. Even in front of the TV in the patients' sitting area there was no one to be seen.

Oh. Today was Tuesday.

The day of the *sandai*, the weekly market. Everybody would go to Puththoor to buy ghee. Going to the sandai used to be like going to a festival for me. That's the way it was for Amma. It was the only day she stepped out of the house. She always wore a *kandaangi seelai,* a sari woven with checks in the fine old style. At home there'd be a smell of garlic around her, or a smell of ghee, or chilli powder, but when she set out for the sandai she'd be fragrantly powdered. Working ceaselessly in the cowshed and the fields and the kitchen had won for her a firm-fleshed body and an upright, swinging gait. Hurrying with my little legs to keep up with her, I'd be so pround of her. I felt that whole world was at her feet when the butter-sellers called "*vaanga! vaanga!*" and she was not enticed by their clamour but smelt and tasted their samples one by one before she said, "This will do. Boil it and give me a kilo." The butter would be boiled down to the proper consistency, with a handful of *murungai* leaves thrown in to crackle and burst their aroma into it. Taken off the fire, it would be strained into a *thookku*. When we went home, swinging that stainless steel pail full of ghee, it felt to me as though we had just bought ourselves a treasure beyond compare, equal in value to a whole kingdom. The next day Appa's favourite *adhirasams* would be prepared without fail. Making what pleased Appa was as good as offering something to God. Just two years ago it was while she was making those adhirasams that she had a heart attack. Seems she died with her fist full of adhirasam dough. I was doing graduate studies in America at the time. By the time I reached home the rites were over. That Appa's wings had been broken was plain to see. Not heeding Appa's repeated protests, I dropped my studies and stayed back in India. And I don't regret it, either. It often occurred to me that Amma would feel I had done right. She'd be at peace in the other world. "Be brave!" was something Amma never told me. "Don't trust men!" was something she had never said. Nor had she openly said, "Every step I take in this house has been won through hard struggle!" But this is what every corner and crevice in the house echoed every day. They tell me to regard with suspicion the affection Appa shows to me.

When I reached the house, Appa was just about to go out.

"I'm going up to Namakkal, amma," he told me. "To buy a new pumpset for the farm. I was just waiting for you to come back home."

"I'll go and get it, Appa. Why do you have to go?"

"What an idea! I have the time for it, so I can go."

"Is Maanikkam driving you there?"

"Yes. Don't worry unnecessarily."

"Did you drink your juice, Appa?"

"Oh yes, 'mma. I'll be going, then or they will close the shop over there."

"All right, get along then, appa. Raasamma, put a bottle of water in the car."

"I've kept it there already, akka," said Maanikkam.

"Drive carefully, Maanikkam," I said, helping Appa get into the car and closing the door. His mind on something or other, Appa smiled distractedly at me. I stood there till the car left, and then turned and went into the house.

Raasmma brought me coffee. "It's because you take care of him like this that he's so lost and helpless when you're not there. I've even asked him, ayya, what'll you do when akka gets married and goes away?" she remarked.

Anger came over me, in an instant. "Raasamma, if you ever talk such stupid rubbish to him like that again, I'll be terribly angry!"

Raasmma gave me a mildly astonished look. "Why, I didn't say anything wrong,' nga!"

"Wrong or right, it is sheer impertinence! Don't talk like that, d'you understand?"

"I won't talk any more, 'nga."

I took my coffee out to the garden and sat down on the bench, my chest still thumping with rage. "Idiot! Idiot!" I cursed her inwardly. " 'Didn't say anything wrong, 'nga?' But why should you be so very bothered about his welfare! For the salary you get all you have to do is boil the rice and dish it out twice daily. What makes you fit to do anything more than that? What wonderful thing are you going to achieve by saying such a thing?"

Abruptly I calmed myself. That was the way Raasamma talked. There was no point getting worked up about it. Nor could I continue to get upset with Shiva for saying: If you don't give up this obstinacy of yours, you're going to stay alone. My dead mother – she was the one with whom I was really furious for having died and left me shouldering what was really her burden.

My mother, who had carried herself like a queen. . . who suddenly slumped againt the courtyard pillar one day at dusk, dying as helplessly as any wandering destitute woman. It was she who had provoked this flaming rage inside me.

And yes, it was strange. Strange that though it was Appa who was responsible for everything, I was not angry with him.

Three

It was not that there wasn't any anger in me against Appa. But it was important to me that he shouldn't, in any way, be dissatisfied with me. Which was extraordinary, really. I didn't want to ask myself why. Nor was there really any need to do so. I knew why I felt that way, and that was what made me so vulnerable, what provoked in me such a desperate desire to prove myself to him.

Whenever I came home after I'd successfully handled a complicated case, I would go to him eager to share my triumph, only to shrink back, rebuffed by the worry-wrinkles suddenly contorting his brow. The way he looked at me, the disappointment hidden in his glance, I remember these making me instantly guilty right from the time I was a child. I'm harried by the fear that my whole life will be spent trying to extricate myself from this disappointment of his that has been flung like a net over my very existence. I understand now why I used to explode with rage when the woman who had given birth to my father jeered, "What is all this reading, di! You're just a girl! A female!"

I always came first in every class at school. Proudly I would show Appa my report card, and a smile would slowly spread over his face. When he ran his fingers gently through my hair it felt like dew falling, it was so gentle, so tender. A hope would sprout; a belief that I had a place in his kingdom after all. And just as quickly as it sprouted, Amma and Paati would throw mud on it and stamp it down.

"Go and show off this degree of yours! Stick it on your forehead! But the fellow who'll hold your hand tomorrow is not going to be impressed! He'll only ask you if you can boil rice! Tell him you've failed in *that* subject, and he won't even come near you!"

I cursed them for saying such words. 'Heartless, pitiless creatures,' I called them, swearing secretly in filthy words. Night after night I drenched my pillow with tears. "I *am* going to college! I *am*!" I told my mother once when I was seventeen, as I sat eating dosais in the kitchen. She laughed as though I had made some kind of joke. Even today, I find it hard to forgive her for this. I've had to do battle for the simplest things – things which could have been so easily granted without any fuss, but which were forever closed off to me because of the obstacles Paati constantly placed in my path. And Amma, too. Like the piper who keeps the pitch for the *nadaswaram* player, she intoned whatever Paati said. Just thinking of it infuriated me.

"This isn't a joke, Amma!" I would say, vehemently, my eyes spilling over, my heart hurting with an indescribable feeling of insult.

"Look here, stop this useless talk," Paati told me. "No need for you to get educated! Nobody here is depending on you to earn or anything. You cannot become a man! So shut up and stay quiet!" The anger and cruelty in her words staggered me. Oh, if I could only have wrung Paati's neck right then! I still remember the feeling of thwarted rage.

I went on a fast of protest, and my father relented. It was decided that I could continue my studies. Amma and Paati had to give in. To me Appa appeared to be the only generous one of the lot, and so I became motivated by a greedy desire to grab his entire attention. But it was not just a longing for his attention, or for his praise. I see now – it was a need to be accepted by him, totally.

Even after I had managed to get an education, and a profession, I was still burdened by that yearning. It was strange and hard to explain to anybody else: I felt rather like Sikhandi in the *Mahabharata* who was neither man nor woman. Paati's well-remembered taunt ("You can't become a man!") still arouses in me a feeling of uselessness, that I'm an in-between creature good for neither this nor that. And that produces a defiant "I'll show you what I can do, just wait and see!" kind of reaction. That was why Shiva laid that curse upon me: that I'll always be "alone".

This loneliness that's been haunting me since my birth – I'm the only one who knows what it is like. That's why it has never been enough for me to be just myself, I need a larger frame. I decided that if I was to create that larger dimension for myself, I had to assert myself. It's not an ordinary desire or dream, it smoulders in me constantly like a fire. It's always there, always burning. I must not hesitate to cast all my other desires into that flame. To incinerate them.

I first became aware of this need one evening. Darkness had just started to spread, as I arrived home suddenly from the hostel in Madras on a short break. If Appa had known I was coming, he would have sent a car to Salem Junction. Throughout the bus journey home I had been entertaining myself with the anticipated surprise I was planning for them. Home grew nearer, and the sheer scent of the earth sent my pulse thrumming, my senses humming. The fields along the highway belonged to my father. They were glistening wet after the rains. Those women transplanting paddy— I knew them! They were from the *keezhtheru* — the lowland quarter where the labourers lived. Exultantly I turned to the woman sitting next to me and said, "That's our field!" She gave me an odd look. "So, you're already married?" she asked. An unnecessary question...but at that moment I was so happy that I didn't feel irritated by it. Every inch...every inch of that expanse of land was familiar to me. All those who worked on it were close to me —close enough for me to call them by their names. One day they were going to install me in Appa's place, and go on with their lives…

I reached home, thinking about how Amma and Paati would rush up and embrace me, and imagining the pleased expression on Appa's face. When I entered the compound, the absence of his parked car was a let down. Muniappan, the gardener showed no surprise, he just nodded a spiritless welcome.

"Where is everybody?" I demanded, hiding my disappointment. He gestured within. The lights were not on although it was growing dark. An emptiness seemed to grip the house, and as I entered I felt my stomach churn, I didn't know why. Was something wrong with Appa's health? Was he in hospital? Was that why the car wasn't there?

"Amma!" I called out, throwing my handbag on the sofa and walking swiftly along the length of the house, switching on the light in room after room. In the inner courtyard, the sunken *mutram* open to the sky, where dark shadows were gliding about in the greying light sat a figure, leaning against the pillar, with legs outstretched into the central space. It took me a while to recognize my mother. Her face was flushed, as though she had been weeping. Beside myself with fear, in that instant of terrible imaginings, I cried, "Amma? What is it, Amma? What happened?" and shook her by the shoulder. Taken unawares, she stared at me, dazed.

"When did you come, di? Did Appa tell you to come?"

"No!" I answered, bewildered. "What's the matter? Is anything wrong with Appa?"

"Him? What can be wrong with HIM?" she said, lowering her head. "Looks so fine he can be offered a seat and given in marriage."

A jest? But a bitterness I had never encountered before revealed itself in that remark. A long-buried hoard of anger. This was an

Amma I did not know. She was not the one who never crossed the line that Appa drew for her, not the wife who had considered it the purpose of her life to please her husband, and only existed within that boundary. Did she have likes and dislikes of her own? I doubted it. Whatever Appa liked suited her. Whatever he did not like, she could do without. For such a woman to talk as she did now was baffling, and infuriating.

"Tell me what the matter is!" I said impatiently. "Don't confuse me."

"Me? I'm confusing you?" she cried out sharply, pushing my hand off her shoulder. Her lips quivered as her anguish forced itself out. "Go and ask your Appa. To sit on a marriage seat – that is what he wants! Arrangements are being made for a second marriage!"

"What!" I said, shaken. It was incredible, it was ridiculous! "For Appa? A second marriage?"

She nodded speechlessly. I suddenly felt like laughing. "Amma, somebody is spinning you a story, and you believe it? Appa is not the kind of person who would ever do such a thing."

Tears gushed from her eyes. "That's what I thought too, di! I swear I never thought he would do such a thing. But it is the truth. People here have done something to his mind. If busybodies keep stirring up things, even a stone will melt. Quite true."

Still it seemed to me to be beyond belief. Preposterous.

"What for? Why a second marriage?" She blew her nose and wiped it with the end of her sari. "Wants a son – a male heir."

Once again I felt shaken. My whole body felt as if it had been set aflame. After so many years? "Till today, in your nineteenth year, this thought that you carry in your mind – that you are my daughter — that's nothing but a made-up story." Is that what he is saying to me? Is he telling me that our relationship has no meaning? I can't believe it. Punishment for not being born a boy. Punishment for not having given birth to a boy. Was it Appa who was doing this? What will he do if the second one also bears only girls? Will he chase her out as well?

Was my father really so cruel? I found it unthinkable. Listening to the neighbours and consenting to a second marriage seemed very degrading to me. Such desperation for a male heir that he could just shake off and push away all the bonds between us… it was a challenge I could never hope to surmount. I was outraged that Amma and I had been left defenceless. She, who had gone around complacently thinking that she was his wife, now lay in a crumpled heap, overcome by shock that the god whom she worshipped had turned into mere clay, and overcome with terror at what lay ahead. The sense of insult was crushing. I looked at her. As I waited for my father to reach home, I could hardly contain my anger.

I don't remember, now, everything I actually said as I shouted at him. The anger, the shock, the grief are what have mostly remained in my memory. What if your second wife doesn't bear a son? What will you do then? Will you marry a third, a fourth, and go on marrying? All the women who have trusted you – will you throw them out into the street? I remember asking him all this. And challenging him, sobbing… "Say, 'You're not my daughter!' Let me hear you say that!" I remember the terrible weariness that came over me, as though I had fought a great war.

At the end of it when Appa told me he had given up the idea of getting married again it didn't make me happy, either. I could not forget the bitterness that had been caused, I couldn't heal the wound. I expected my mother to be sensitive to the insult done to her, but she clung to him even more closely than before. As though the paradise she had lost had been restored to her. She heaved a sigh of relief. Her release from the fear of being abandoned made her feel a debt of gratitude to Appa all her life.

But how could Appa ever have consented to such a plan in the first place? The question troubles me, even now.

Appa had not yet returned from Namakkal. I picked up the TIME magazine from his table and started to read it. I was immersed in an interesting article on the O.J. Simpson case when Paavaayee called, "Will you come to the pujai, Amma?"

I looked up. Paavaayee had bathed and washed her hair. Her sari had been washed, and she looked bright and fresh. The drying golden paste of turmeric on her cheeks and the big vermilion dot on her forehead gave her an auspicious glow.

"What pujai?" I asked, still in the grip of the magazine article.

"Today is new moon, isn't it, `nga?" Paavaayee reminded me. Everyone's here. All of us are waiting for you."

The article had completely taken hold of me. Reluctantly I got up, saying "Oh, all right, you go on, I'm coming." Instructing Raasamma to lock the door I set out for the clinic, and by the time I reached the garden behind it all of them, from the gardener Muniappan to Meenatchi herself, were standing in god-fearing attitudes around the stone symbol of Mangamma's spirit. Paavaayee had given the stone a bath, too. Smeared with turmeric, it bore a broad red *kumkumam* mark. On its head was jasmine, strands of it rolled into a ball. They had carefully propped up coconut fronds around the small, flat earthen oil-lamp to keep it from going out. The offering of milk and bananas and coconut, the fragrant smoke from a piece of *akil*-wood – together they produced the illusion that Mangamma was no mere imaginary being. With Meenatchi raising an eerie ululation and Paavaayee setting aflame a bit of camphor, the face took on a more-than-human radiance in the surrounding darkness. Everybody slapped themselves submissively on their cheeks. In a loud voice Paavayee called out, "Mangamma Thayee!" She muttered unintelligible words, folded her hands and offered prayers with brimming eyes, the tears rolling down her cheeks. Those tears, the melodrama that these people had created for themselves, the hysteria that they summoned up around it – in the beginning all this used to annoy me. They're the sort who cry at movies, I used to say, exasperated. But in the last few years I feel as if I have changed, and become one of them. My life in the city, the acquisition of higher education, a comfortable existence without financial worries – it seems to me that these fragile layers in which I am wrapped are slowly being removed, one by one. When they cry out "Mangamma Thayee!" with tearful eyes, I understand that it is for the family of womankind in general.

O woman who bore me
If I told you my woe
Your bright golden face
Would lose all its glow

It was just like that time, when the old woman sang and everybody wept. When Mangamma climbed up her husband's bier and lay herself down upon it to make herself a burning log "for his sake", she hadn't died happily. These women knew that.

Kamalini used to talk about the royal women of Rajasthan. She said that in the last century the women who were about to commit sati pressed their oil-smeared palms on the walls as they passed along the corridor of the women's quarters. The prints were still there, she said. "And what is the meaning of it?" she would ask, in a professional tone. That in Rajasthan, too, many Paavayees have existed and many Mangammas. That for all those who sacrificed their lives with their mouths shut, there were those who would mourn them, with open, wailing mouths. That must be the answer to Kamalini's question. A memory surfaced, suddenly – of the black man who was accused of murdering his ex-wife and her lover, and was finally pronounced innocent and set free. Was he really innocent, or had he escaped because of the whole question of blacks against whites? Paavaayee wouldn't understand the problem of colour, but she was quite capable of an empathy intense enough to set up a stone to honour O.J.'s ex-wife. The offering of milk and fruit was distributed to everyone. Actually, a kind of peace hung over the place. All the faces looked as though they had unburdened themselves. As though they had set down their little bundles of sins. Mangamma would protect them all. Including me.

Four

As Muniappan hovered protectively close to me the women scattered and fell in behind Paavayee, following her as though they were possessed. Every time I witness this fortnightly ritual, I'm amazed at this superb emotional release they have created for themselves. No form of therapy can match such sublimation. Spellbound, they offer up flaming camphor to an imagined spirit, weeping copiously, and it is as though all their problems dissolve in tears.... Watching them walk away after the worship, chattering and laughing happily, it occurs to me that Amma must have created some such outlet for herself, without my knowledge. How else could she have just gulped everything down and gone on right up to her last breath, making adirasams for Appa, after what he did?

I hesitate, these days, to explain away all Amma's actions in terms of her economic dependency. What must have had a greater impact on her was the shock of finding out that her love was being set aside. And so she seems to me to have responded by disarming him completely with that same extraordinary love of hers. Ultimately that was the way she established her right over him, because that was the only way she knew.

A whole generation lies between Amma and myself. Her compulsions and inhibitions don't exist for me. I'm an educated woman. I can earn not just my own living, but enough to sustain a family for the next two generations. Yet I realize that between Amma's yearning to justify her existence in some way, and my wanting some kind of approval, if not quite appreciation, for every step I take, there isn't really that much difference. Sometimes this awareness throws me off balance. Amma's was a lonely struggle. Maybe that is how mine must be too. "You'll remain all alone, in the end." Shiva's words came back to me once again. I resolved to myself: if that's the only way I can win, then loneliness is no big thing. *You have your goal, and I have mine. You say my way is not the world's way. I say I'll make the world go my way. You don't want to go this way? Well then, just go away!*

"What 'mma, Ayya has not yet come, 'nga?" Startled, I came back to myself. A panicky feeling clutched at the pit of my stomach. No sign of Appa's car. My wristwatch showed nine o'clock. In worry and exasperation I said, "I told him I'd go and buy whatever he wanted! I said, 'Don't go wandering around.' But he didn't listen, he just went off!"

"But it's a pump set that he has gone to buy, no?" asked Muniappan.

"So what? Can't I buy it?"

"What, amma? How can he leave such jobs to you, 'nga?"

Irritated, I didn't answer.

Muniappan pronounced judgement on the affair: "Supposing a son-in-law comes, then he can be asked to do such things."

I laughed. "You think some fellow will turn up just to do Appa's odd jobs? To 'do this thing!' and 'get that thing!'"

"Odd-job man? Is that what I said?" retorted Muniappan, offended. "When there is no male member in a household, then it is for the son-in-law to take on the responsibility."

A mistake, I thought, even to have started this conversation. He seemed to have made up his mind that this must be the rule in any household without a male member. Apparently this was what all the servants discussed in their spare time. Raasamma heard us talking and opened the door.

"Periayya hasn't come yet, akka?" she enquired.

"He'll come," I said, as though I was reassuring myself. "Maybe he stopped for dinner in Namakkal. You go and eat, Raasamma."

"It's all right, 'kka, I can wait."

"He will come," said Muniappan encouragingly. "Perhaps the car is giving trouble." Seeing him preparing to squat on his haunches outside the door, I told him, "You can go, Muniappan, it's getting late."

"That's all right. I'll just sit here till Ayya comes," he said, staunchly. "You go and eat, 'nga. Go and lie down."

'Now that this fellow has made up his mind that it's his job as a man to be my bodyguard, it's impossible to move him from this spot!' I thought, and went inside. When Appa was a child, this man's father had been the gardener. He and Appa may even have been playmates at one time. But so far he has never overstepped the limits set for him in showing his respect. Underlying both Amma's feelings towards Appa, and these people's feudal loyalty, I sense the same principle. It is something beyond a mere indebtedness for the food one eats, it's a barrier they have constructed for their own protection. Is it against a fear that even an edifice of gratitude can be razed to the ground?

Realizing Raasamma wouldn't eat if I didn't, I went to the table, made a show of eating and rose, saying, "Cover the food and leave it on the table for Appa. You go and eat, Raasamma."

"I'll just wait for another half hour, amma."

"As you like," I told her and went to my room.On the TV in the hall there was a re-run of an old MGR film, and she was immersed in it. Her mother had been a `devotee' of MGR, Raasamma had told me. Her father had died at a young age. "My amma never talked about my appa. For her, it was always only MGR …she had his photo everywhere in the house," she would tell me, with a chuckle. It surprises her, now, that nobody in the neighbourhood took it the `wrong way'. If I say to her that MGR worship acted as an outlet for the sexual frustrations of poor women in Tamil Nadu, she would probably be outraged.

I lay down in my bedroom and opened the issue of TIME magazine once again. Refusing to settle on it, my mind began to leap about. First there were thoughts of Appa, and then all of a sudden Shiva emerged, popping up on the bounding crest of a wave of memory ...I couldn't understand where it came from, that thought of Shiva. The words that Muniappan had babbled must have stirred up my subconscious. But there was more to it. Whenever I was overcome by loneliness Shiva's words kept coming back to me, as though they were the prophecy of some disembodied spirit. It made me very angry—what right did he have, anyway, to curse me like that?

He hadn't been in touch after that. Not after saying such a thing to me, that Sunday evening, on that beach in Chennai.

I hadn't expected him to turn up in Chennai at that two-day seminar I'd gone to attend. After all, it was in Hyderabad that he worked. But suddenly there he was and at the sight of him my heart had thumped joyously, and my cheeks were hot. No denying that. He was happy to see me, too —his face clearly showed it. And this was after our last meeting when we'd felt that the relationship between us had forever ended.

"Hallo, Mano!" He sounded very natural, as though nothing had happened. "How are you? Is your father all right?"

I thought he may have got married, and when he told me he wasn't it gave me a meaningless feeling of gratification.

"And you?" he asked eagerly.

"No," I said. For a while he seemed to be paying attention to the discussion going on in front of us. Then he turned and said, "I have to talk to you, Mano. This evening, let's go to the beach and talk, will you come?"

"I'll come," I said, without hesitation.

Then I added, cautiously, "Has there been any change in your ideas?"He lowered his head. "I keep having thoughts of you. I feel I must talk to you. To make them clearer."

It seemed to me that he was not lying. Which meant I had won. There was a tiny feeling of elation.

"I have no objection," I smiled.

"Thank you," he said, and pressed my hand, openly emotional.

It was after my MBBS while I was doing my MD that I had got to know Shiva. A friendship that began in the library, it broke free of my self-imposed restrictions and grew to the point where everybody began to talk about us, making obvious connections. Home on vacation, it gave me a shock to find that the talk had entered Amma's kitchen. Paati was still alive then. I felt her eyes following me suspiciously.

"Why Paati, why are you looking at me like that?" I asked her, smiling.

"There is something strange about you," she announced.

"What's strange?"

"That walk of yours – it's not nice."

I laughed out loud, "Why? I'm walking just as I always do!"

"Nowadays you don't just walk. You bounce! And for nothing at all you start laughing."

Again I laughed. "Why, Paati, is that wrong at my age?"

"Think you're at a very young age, di? Twenty-five years! If you jump about like a young girl, of course it will look strange."

I looked at Amma. Abruptly she looked down and began to dice vegetables. For no reason at all, they were putting me down! These women were putting a dampner on all my enthusiasm! "Just what are you thinking, all of you?" I shouted, enraged. "Here I have come, tongue gone dull with hostel food, after dreaming endlessly about coming! And when a girl comes home, all you can do is to find fault with her, `You're laughing! You're jumping!'

Chhe! What kind of people are you?" My voice had risen to a scream.

"You can laugh, you can jump, why you can even dance if you like! But don't you dare drag the family's prestige into the bazaar!" Paati shouted back.

At once I became wary. "Nobody's prestige has been dragged into the bazaar! Don't just say whatever comes into your head! If you talk like that I won't come home for the next holidays!" I shouted angrily, and stalked off to my room.

I could not weep. Instead I felt like laughing. My secret was out – the private treasure I'd been hoarding up was laid bare! Because just as Paati said, I had indeed changed! My nerves, my very blood vessels were taut, they were chiming in tune and making glorious music. Behind my closed eyelids like a scene from a movie Shiva and I were floating together. Right at the centre of a deluge... with music all around us. There was nobody but him and me. How marvellous it was, our private world!

That privacy was shattered by my mother's voice. Opening my eyes, I saw her standing there gazing intently at me: The trepidation, the sorrow, and the bewilderment in that gaze did something indescribable to me. The smile that had come naturally to my lips vanished. Why were these women trying to punish me for experiencing what they had missed out in their lives? Anger came, hot and fast.

"You've also come to give me advice, have you?" I said, bitterly. "What has happened that Paati should howl like that? As though somebody were dead!"

"Ush... talk softly, di," said Amma sternly. Then she sat quiet, her eyes still fixed on me.

"What is it, Amma? What's the matter?" I said, uneasily.

"Nothing...somebody said that...you have got friendly with some person in the city. My daughter will not do anything wrong, I know. I haven't come to say anything about that. But I just want to remind you about one thing: You shouldn't blunder into some mess and just give up whatever right you have in this house. Don't give up your fort! ...I'm not an educated woman. I don't know how to explain things more than this."

Amma got up and left, as if to say that there was nothing more to be said. I felt as though she had given me a thorough shaking. At first I felt a blazing anger. How dare she barge into my secret world? Why, it was emotional blackmail! The tears came, in furious bursts.

But by the time I went back to Chennai I was surprised to find myself thinking very differently about the whole thing.

I don't quite comprehend how I came to believe that Shiva would acquiesce to my conditions. But the incredulous look on his face when I told him about them made me understand that the story was now all finished. I saw that he would never understand how I felt. When he had caught hold of my hands and huskily pleaded, " I love you, Mano!" it had given me a strange feeling — that something not quite real was happening. And when I answered, "If it is true that you love me, then our life should be the way I want it to be," it seemed such a silly answer — like in the old 'raja-rani' stories, when the imperious princess imposes her will on her beggarly suitor. "If this is love, then sacrifice is a part of it, Shiva!" I told him, with a smile.

"So, why don't you be the one who does the sacrificing?" had been Shiva's retort.

"I don't love you quite that much!" was the answer to that one, but I hesitated to come out with it: I couldn't tell him about the much greater sacrificial fire in my life, one that I was building up very carefully, which had the power to turn to ashes all other attachments, and all romance. It would have brought my image plummeting down in his eyes. It frightened me that I couldn't love anybody completely. This inadequacy made me feel weak.

And yet my body was in shameless need of his maleness... craving for him to hold my hand a little longer.

Apparently sensing this weakness, he caressed my cheek. "Every day you're becoming lovelier," he said. "You and I...how will it be when we live together...that's what I dream about every day," he said amorously. But I shook myself free, and drew back, declaring, "I can't agree to any other arrangement, Shiva. You must understand my situation." That I could speak like this, that I hadn't lost my senses, gave me confidence, and a kind of calm.

"Not a single fellow will come and live here, in this village!" What Kamalini had said was true and I knew it. No one would do it, apart from some fellow among our relations with an eye on the property, and I didn't want to marry any of them. "If you keep rejecting everybody like this what will happen?" said Appa once, helplessly, after I had spurned yet another suitor.

"So, just let me be the way I am. If it is any bother to you, just tell me, 'pa!"

"How can you like this forever, 'ma?"

It would throw him into a terrible confusion, for a time. On several occasions I would have to change the direction of his thoughts, firmly telling him, "Talk about something else, Appa!" But I knew how this whole question burned at him like a fire that would go out only when he had got me married off. I felt ashamed that I had not succeeded in liberating my father from his insecurities about me, and his perplexities.

I heard his car draw up at the gate, came abruptly to my senses and hurried out. The car had come to a stop, Maanikkam was opening the back door and Appa was getting out, exhaustion writ on his face. I rushed to him and took his hand.

"What Appa, why so late?"

"Come inside, I'll tell you," he said wearily.

"What Maanikkam, there's nothing wrong with Appa, is there?"

"Anything wrong with the car?" queried Muniappan.

"Nothing like that," answered Manikkam.

Feeling slightly relieved, I followed Appa inside. Raasamma switched off the TV, put on the fan, and stood ready with cool water for Appa to drink. Appa took it and downed it in a single gulp. Leaning back on the sofa, he said, "The place I went to—it so happened I had to attend a death there. That's why it got so late."

"Who?" I asked, bewildered.

"My friend Pandurangan – you know? Suddenly in Namakkal last night he had a heart attack, and died. I heard about it and went there. What complete confusion! Nobody to light the funeral pyre!"

"Doesn't he have children?"

"Just one daughter," said Appa.

Five

It was close to midnight. Quite without warning my father had just dealt me a blow that felt like an accusation. Issuing from him as he sat there, a figure bowed down with fatigue and despair, the words attacked me, they made me stagger. They meant: You are a zero! Appa had seized this moment as the most opportune one to insult me.

It felt like a slap across the face. For a moment or two my tongue lay immobile in my mouth, unable to stir. Then I asked, "Just a daughter? What does that mean? Wasn't she born to them?" I could sense my voice shaking, soaring in pitch. I had no strength to control it.

Awaiting Appa's instructions, Maanikkam and Muniappan stood by the door and Raasamma by the dining table. Abruptly Appa looked up at me. Then he turned towards the door and said, "You can leave, Maanikkam… Tell Muniappan to leave also."

When Raasamma returned from locking the front door after them, he told her, "I must have a bath. No food. Only two bananas and some hot milk, that is enough," and rose.

"All right,'nga, 'yya."

Raasamma's gaze, so obviously sympathetic, was fixed on me, and it made me feel very uneasy. Everybody seemed to be using this sympathy to dig a pit for me. Asking Appa that question in front of these people had been stupid, I thought. He hadn't answered. He had walked past me, and was now climbing up the stairs.

I knew how exhausted he was but I followed him, determined to get an answer. And then, in a flash I understood the reason for his tiredness. He had lit the funeral pyre for his luckless friend, who did not have a male heir, and whose male relations shrank from the ritual implications of lighting a sonless person's pyre. There was pollution involved, there were taboos. Once again I felt guilt being thrust on me, and it outraged me. Quickly overtaking Appa, I went into his room and switched on the light. Avoiding my eyes, he began to unbutton his shirt, saying, "You go and lie down, amma."

"You have not answered my question."

Appa gave a faint smile.

"That was a very silly question, amma!"

"Why?" I said, vehemently.

Without looking at me, Appa went towards the bathroom, saying, "The daughter is married and has gone to another house. She does not have the right to light the funeral pyre. For ages people have believed certain things, they have been observing certain customs. To go and question such a thing is stupid."

Appa went into the bathroom and locked the door. In a few moments the sound of the shower came through the door. No use standing there any more...I went to my room and lay down.

What if the daughter had not married? Not gone away to another house? Would she have lit the funeral pyre then? Perhaps Appa was giving me a gentle hint.

"For ages people have believed certain things."

But do *you* believe them? Will you give me that right? When you are lying there lifeless and dead, will the world make me a wretched female with nothing to call her own? Will they make you a helpless corpse with nobody to cremate you? Will we both be victim to that humiliation? Will you consent to it? Say then that it's foolish to question society?

What Appa had said today, and his unsatisfactory half-smile

made me feel badly let down. I imagined him standing under the shower and thinking: it's just to escape this kind of thing happening to me that I agreed to get married a second time...That he could not recognize his predicament as completely preposterous made me furious. Instantly there was a memory of Amma. I remembered her sitting on the edge of my bed and the anxiety in her gaze.

"You shouldn't blunder into some mess and just give up whatever right you have in this house. Don't lose your fort!"

The memory of those words shook me in a new way. What was the right that Amma meant? Didn't she know about all these rituals and customs? Of course Amma knew. When she had said, "I'm not an educated woman. I'm not going to teach you." It meant, "Daughter, get smart!" Mine was a right that could not be argued in court by a lawyer, and won. Amma knew that too. That was how smart my uneducated mother was. But she just wasn't in a position to ask the question: why all this guile to obtain what should be given naturally?

I closed my eyes. "Appa, I will be the one to light your pyre!" I said loudly. As I tossed and turned, the night scattered into fragments of a dream—appa, all stretched out, a corpse. Holding a flaming torch, I run toward him, I approach him. To set him on fire. The corpse rises and runs away. I give relentless chase . "I will light it! No one else! I will be the one to do so!"

When I opened my eyes in the morning the sunlight invading the room struck me sharply on the face and I rose with a jerk. The vestiges of the dream persisted as scraps of memory, and my body ached as though it was exhausted with running. Glancing out of the window I saw that the spot where the car was parked was empty. Appa must have left for Namakkal. By the time he returned after performing Pandurangan's obsequies, it would be noon.

I couldn't tell him — "Don't go, Appa, this running about isn't good for you!" He was a person who deemed it imperative not only to be present but to take an active part in all events, happy or sad, that took place in the households of relations and close friends. "Only then will people come to us when we need them." Now with Pandurangan's death his behaviour took on a new meaning. Appa had been making people aware of his own need. When his time came...*I too, only have a daughter. So when I close my eyes, it is you who must bring me ashore. What I did for Pandurangan you must do for me.*

Bring me ashore. There was a sound of somebody coming up the stairs. I must be going quite mad, I thought. Hurrying to the bathroom I went in and shut the door. Lowering my face into the washbasin, I splashed it with water. When I raised it and looked into the mirror, it still looked terrible. Searching for something that wasn't there, I saw Paati's face. "You can't become a man," she said. I wanted to stab that face. To gouge it out.

The hermaphrodite Sikhandi must have felt like this when Bhishma told him:

O you who lack manhood! A disgrace
It is for me to fight you, face to face!

Sikhandi must have felt this same rage. He bore the insult, retorting:

It is in this guise alone that I will indeed
Vanquish you, and in my goal succeed!

Paati says, "You're not Sikhandi. You are a girl. Just an ordinary girl. You, vanquish? Why you're not even fit to light your father's funeral pyre! You're just a cypher!"

"I will light it! Only I will light Appa's funeral pyre!

Suddenly I realized, with a shock and a surge of shame, that I was thinking more about Appa's death than he was himself! What was the matter with me? Really, I was just a very ordinary woman. All my learning, my degree, and my profession, and the crowd of grateful patients chanting "You are a goddess, thayee!" had become meaningless. Paati's argument had been just that: nothing that I did could make me a man.

I looked in the mirror. *I don't want to become a man.*

Paati was no longer to be seen there.

When I went down, all ready to leave for the nursing home, Raasamma was waiting with tiffin.

"Ayya has left for Namakkal, akka," she informed me. "He told me to tell you that it will be afternoon by the time he comes back."

"Right," I said briefly. To let her know that I didn't want to talk further I spread out the newspaper and began to read as I ate tiffin. Otherwise Raasamma would have pleaded not only Appa's cause but that of all those people who had gone around desperately searching for somebody to set alight Pandurangan's corpse. Raaamma was four years younger than me. Five years ago her husband died of an intestinal ulcer caused by drink. Last year Thangaraju who had a cycle repair shop in town wanted to marry her. Raasamma got terribly flustered. "Tell me if that's what you want, and I will arrange the marriage," I told her. But she shed tears of guilt, as though it were a sin against the gods. "A second marriage is not permissible!" declared her family, putting a fullstop to the whole idea. Just as her mother had coped with her frustration with the aid of pictures of MGR, this woman smeared holy ash on her forehead, seated herself before the TV, saying. "This is in my fate, akka." If she had married Thangaraju any girl-child conceived in her womb would have been my responsibility. I would have had to listen weakly to her tearful plea, "Must she suffer what I suffer, Akka?"

So let her be destroyed. Let the female sex be wiped out. She doesn't need to feel this humiliation that I undergo. Wipe her out.

"Isn't it a crime under the law, Mano?"

Don't talk to me about the law, it has no meaning at all. Society is one thing, the law is another. But here law is just what society decides. Does your law say that a son —*a puttiran* — is essential for an escape from the hell they call *Put*? Among our people that is the law. Even my own father believes it. He searched for somebody to light the funeral pyre of his friend who died leaving behind 'just' a daughter. Maybe he's making some kind of arrangement – picking out some surrogate son – who knows?

Actually not a line of the newspaper had impressed itself on my consciousness. I finished the idlis, drank my coffee in a single gulp and rose, saying, "Today I have many cases. Send my food to the nursing home."

"All right, `nga,`kka," she said, giving me a doubtful look. Paying no heed, I set off. If she had concluded that I was trying to avoid seeing Appa in the afternoon, I didn't care.

The sight of the woman waiting at the nursing home gate did not perk me up, as it usually did. "Vanakkam, `kka," said Shanbagam. As always her smile was measured and submissive. I had never seen her parting her lips or showing her teeth in a free and open laugh.

Shanbagam's husband had been a master mason when the nursing home was being built. When her husband died suddenly, she had become utterly distraught. It was I who had got her the job at the site. She was now a master mason in her own right, and yet her appearance remained unchanged – that frugal smile, and those signs of widowhood on her person. "That's why my brothers and sisters accept me," she had explained to me one day.

"What is it, Shanbagam? How are you?"

"I'm all right, akka. Just thought I would come and see you."

She was not the kind who 'just' turned up to see anybody.

"Let me see if there's any urgent case waiting. Sit down," I told her, and went in.

There were only the usual gynae cases. Some uteruses failing to conceive. No emergencies. I went back to Shanbagam.

"What's the problem, Shanbagam?" I asked her.

"It's nothing, `kka," she murmured, her face lowered. Then with a swift movement she seized hold of my hand. "Akka, I have come because I trust only you!" Her voice oozed misery.

I was used to this kind of scene. But I hadn't expected it from Shanbagam.

"How many months?" I said wearily.

"Just two."

"Then there's no problem!" I exclaimed bitterly. "Why can't you just—leave it all to…to God, or whoever – Shivaney! As they all say, and just get married, Shanbagam?"

She began to cry.

"All right, all right, don't cry. I'm not asking you anything. I'll help you to get rid of it. But from now on you'd better be careful."

With her face still lowered, she took the prescription from me and left the room. I felt very sorry for her. Very likely she was less than thirty years old. She had a fresh glow to her. Even if society had decreed that a lonely life was to be her lot, could a fence be built around a woman who worked within sight of several men? I remember her shrieking when her husband died. I remember how it had struck me as odd that there was more rage than sorrow in that scream. "How dare you leave me like this!" was what came out. As if she had been cruelly cheated.

Yesterday when Pandurangan lay dead, I wonder if his wife's weeping also expressed such frustration? It must have, though the reason for it would probably not have been clear to those gathered there. Because she had failed to bear a son, the death of her husband suddenly brought into glaring light the hollow lie of her married life. Nobody would have realized that it was her being laid bare like that which caused such a violence of grief.

And Appa? The death of his friend who left no son and heir, what kind of impact was it having on him? It made me very anxious. Mechanically I examined all the cases and wrote out prescriptions. I instructed Meenatchi that no cases for scanning would be taken up today. When a couple of patients beseeched me to have their uteruses scanned at once, as though they would lose their minds if they didn't find out right away if the child inside was a girl or a boy, I shouted angrily: "Go away! This is not a place for parrot-astrologers! Don't keep coming here and standing around! By having the scan done today instead of tomorrow, the female in the womb isn't going to turn into a male! Come back tomorrow!"

Even Meenatchi cringed at the noise I made. She hurried and got me coffee without my having to ask for it. "Today's post," she said, and put the letters on my table. I didn't have the spirit even to glance at them today. I shuffled them listlessly like a deck of cards.

Shiva's handwriting caught my eye. In the state I was in, it provoked no response whatsoever in me. That was a surprise.

Six

"Therefore, do your duty, O Partha, looking upon it as sacrifice," says Krishna on the small screen. A mask of blue smeared on his face, he recites a verse in Sanskrit. The TV Arjuna, who is already floundering, caught on the horns of a dilemma between duty and attachment, seems to be even more confounded by the Sanskrit. Smiling, Krishna continues, "The humiliation of Draupadi was not just an insult to one person that it may be pardoned. It was the humiliation of all womankind! Arouse yourself to anger against a society which gloats over such a shameful spectacle. Do battle! Wreak havoc!"

Click! Raasamma changed the channel in the middle of Krishna's exhortation on behalf of the feminist cause.

Suddenly there was Sivaji Ganesan, the character actor, in a scene from an old movie. Brandishing a bottle of Black and White he was declaiming, "I am a coward! That is why I drink and try to forget myself. A coward! That's why I flee in terror from my wife and go to a prostitute."

Raasamma looked at me and laughed. "Did you hear that, `nga? A fine story, isn't it? Says he's a coward. Says that's why he does bad things."

"Why did you change the channel?"

"Oh, were you watching the *Mahabharatha*, akka? I'm sorry…I can't understand that Tamil, that's why I…" Another click and Arjuna was back. Still in a dilemma. "What causes the destruction of dharma?" he wants to know, and Krishna tells him:

"The destruction of dharma occurs because man is not free from delusion."

"Who will understand such talk?" muttered Raasamma.

"Do you know the *Mahabharatha* story, Raasamma?"

"I don't know all that, `nga."

"The story of Panchali?"

"That one I know. The Bommallattam people used to hold their puppet shows near our village. I saw it then, the `Curse of Draupadi'. Poor woman, with five husbands and not even one could protect her from that wicked fellow who tried to shame her in public ! And the Nalla Thangaal story—that good sister with seven selfish brothers, all too stingy to help her when her children are starving and her husband is dying. The shows used to last all night. Do you know, akka, every single woman who came to watch would cry and cry!"

I remembered my mother. The Bommallattam performances took place during the summer holidays. We had to beg and plead with Appa before he would give us permission to go and watch. They would place a special chair for Amma in front of the puppet box, but she would always refuse and would sit on the large striped cotton *jamukaalam* mat with everyone else. The peasants' wives would sit a little way off, but somehow the distance between them would disappear a few minutes after the show began, as Nalla Thangaal's sorrow and Draupadi's agony took hold of everybody.

"Bommallattam is not meant to be watched sitting on a chair," said Amma once.

"Why?" I asked her.

"Look at it from here," she said, pulling me down beside her. With my head on her lap I looked at the stage. The men who stood behind and animated the puppets came into view. From that day on I stopped looking at the puppets and began to watch the men behind the scene. Transformed into Nalla Thangaal and

Draupadi, the puppeteers lived their humiliation and their grief. I found it astonishing that they shed real tears. The miracle of the puppeteer becoming one with his puppet would throw me into a kind of daze.

"I, too, do my duty, Parthaa," Krishna was saying.

"But Kesava..." dithered Arjuna once again, when the electricity went off, and he had to shut up. Both men disappeared from the screen.

Chuckling, Raasamma got up. "By the time the power comes on again, Arjuna's confusion will be all cleared up! Shall I get–you some coffee, 'kka?"

"Yes please," I said, smiling.

How nice if I were in Raasamma's place! Apart from the fact that her husband has died, she had no problems. Nothing that could cause her any agitation or confusion. Perhaps she was so carefree because she had no family ties of any kind. You couldn't, of course, say that she had chosen this life of her own free will, but it was a path that had already been laid down, and it had no entanglements. A life in which doubts had no place. The decision she had taken was, in fact, intended to forestall doubt.

I could have been like Raasamma. I need not have resisted Paati and insisted on getting educated. I need not have earned a bad name for myself by having to refuse every offer of marriage because no man was as educated as I was!

"You shouldn't blunder into some mess and let whatever right you have in this house slip out of your hands."

Just to counter Amma's riddle, I needn't have dragged in a person who said he loved me, and then watched him dangle between his expectations of marriage and the conditions I wanted to impose. Like a flash came the memory of Shiva's letter...I had not even opened it. I'd taken note of the fact that it was Shiva's handwriting on the envelope and then I had put it in the table drawer to read later — and then forgotten all about it! Because there were no urgent cases I had not even been to the clinic. What could he have written?

Desire raised its head, but barely had it surfaced before it subsided and was drowned. After I had made known my conditions to him, letters from him had stopped. I was conscious of an anger underlying that silence. Magnanimously I forgave it as being quite natural. I knew that there were many would-be bridegrooms among my marriageable but uneducated kinsmen who were ready and waiting to give in to all my conditions just because I was a rich man's daughter. It was precisely this that made me feel a kind of painful gratification that Shiva was angry with me.

On sleepless nights, when my body burned with the need for his embrace, I tried to make peace with it, telling myself, "There's no other way for me!" Women asked me to destroy the females in their wombs, pleading, "There's no other way for me!" Our epics and legends say that a woman who wants to achieve anything at all must renounce not only sexual desire, but every sign of femaleness. And so women poet-saints like the great Auvaiyaar, and Karaikkaal Ammaiyaar renounced the full glory of their youth, not wishing to be distracted from their spiritual goals. Kannagi plucked out her breast and flung it at the doomed city of Madurai, burning it to ashes. Andaal threatened to pluck out hers if her divine lover delayed their union

Funny how, without going to any such lengths, Raasamma and I had taken on the ochre of renunciation. Our outlets for the sacrificial impulse were different, that was all. The TV screen for her, the scan screen for me.

My eyes seemed to whirl and wobble as sleep came over me. I stretched my legs out comfortably on the sofa and sank little by little into a shoreless darkness.

Raasamma is standing next to the scan screen, wearing my white coat. "This is the uterus," she demonstrates. "See that so-small thing, that is the foetus. Already the legs and arms have sprouted—see the fingers all spread out, like peacock feathers! Look! There's the penis! Just see how it is already sticking out so proudly!" Raasamma laughs uproariously. "We don't need it, akka!" she says to me. "Give the injections! We don't need it, akka."

"Akka—"

I awoke with a start. The telephone was ringing. Raasamma stood there innocently, with a cup of coffee in her hand. No white overall. "Did you drop off to sleep, Akka?" I yawned and reached for the phone.

"Hallo, Mano?"

Even in that dreamy haze my heart stopped beating for a second. Blood vessels spurted warmth from my feet upwards to the tips of my ears.

Getting a hold on myself I replied, "Hallo, Shiva."

"How are you, Mano?" His intimate tone made me feel weak. What had he written in that letter?

"I am fine, Shiva, how about you?"

"Didn't you get my letter?"

The eagerness in his voice made me falter slightly. "What letter?"

"I wrote you a letter. You must have received it?"

"Yesterday was Saturday. They may not have delivered it. It may come tomorrow. What is it about?"

"You'll know when you read it."

"Why don't you tell me what's in it?"

"No need for that."

Suddenly I was irritated at the way he spoke, so reluctant to commit himself. Perhaps a marriage had been arranged for him. Or he had decided to pay a "girl-viewing" visit, with the idea of having his marriage arranged. Was he going to use that possibility as his final weapon in the stalemate between us?

"As you like," I said. "Where are you speaking from?"

"From Hyderabad. What are you doing now?"

"Me? I'm watching the *Mahabharatha* on TV. 'Do your duty,' Krishna was saying. And the current went off!"

It sounded as though he was laughing lightly. The two of us seemed to be fumbling for words. Flurried as I was by the thought that he might put the phone down, I actually couldn't find anything to say.

"Do you get so much free time that you can actually watch TV?"

"It's Sunday! All the women are at home serving their husbands and fussing over them. And there aren't any emergency cases."

"Why do you hate men, Mano?"

"Hate? Who says so? Doesn't my whole business depend on men?"

He laughed out loud.

"It's that profession of yours. That's what is making you hate men."

"When you have already decided that I hate them, what's there for me to say?"

"Well, you can try to change my opinion."

That he was saying all this just to prolong the conversation gave me a small thrill of satisfaction. With it came a feeling of amazement. What was he trying to tell me?

"I have never tried to make other people think well of me, Shiva. I'll only be myself. I can't be different."

"I know that!"

"Then why all this argument?"

"All right then, no argument. Enough if you say you are not disgusted – I'll be happy."

It was then that I felt a real urge to know what he had written in his letter. Something in his tone suggested an eagerness to make amends. "Okay, read the letter tomorrow and let me know what you think." He said.

"What about?"

"Why should I tell you?"

"Okay, don't tell me!" I laughed.

"I'll speak to you later." The smile was still on my face when I put the receiver down. I felt quite elated. Raasamma handed me the coffee. Quickly downing it, I slipped on my chappals and told her, "I'm just going to the clinic."

By the time I had reached the examination room, opened the drawer and taken out the letter, my hands were shaking. A woman approaching thirty, to be overcome by sentiment like a girl of fifteen! It felt shameful and quite peculiar. "You hate men!" says the idiot. Would he say then that this agitation is just a chemical reaction?

There was a deliberate quality to the handwriting on the blue envelope, with its chains of interwoven letters. Composing myself, I sat down, very straight and solemn. Picking up the paper cutter I neatly slit open the envelope. The letter was in English. He had commenced with the words "My dearest". Stupidly my hair stood on end all over my body. Something turned over and knotted itself in the pit of my belly.

"Whenever I think of you, that is the kind of feeling I get. I cannot think of anybody closer or dearer to me than you. I cannot even imagine somebody else as my life's companion. That you were making a complicated thing out of something very simple did make me angry with you, it is true. But the more I think of you, the more I am able to understand your thoughts and your worries. I am ready to accept your conditions. Why? Because I have realized that my life will not be complete without you. I'll wait to hear from you."

I wanted to laugh out loud. All the examinations I had written successfully so far were as nothing to this triumph. This was the man who had tried to terrify me two months ago, with the threat "You will always be alone." I had seen it for what is was: an empty threat! A bluff! As though not having a man to share my life would make me like some kind of stunted, blasted tree.

And yet, when Appa closed his eyes forever would I have to spend the remainder of my days sitting with Raasamma in front of the TV? The fear of that happening often came home to me in my weaker moments. It occurs to me that even now, in the twenty-first century, when the need for the union of male and female for the sole purpose of procreation is a thing of the past, the sheer maleness of a man, and intimacy with him, might give life if not a wholeness, at least some kind of meaning. My heart tells me that conflicting views and values are just what give life its flavour.

And how bored I am with people around me saying "Yes, `nga! All right, `nga!" all the time.

"I am ready to accept your conditions." How had this change come about? "I cannot accept anybody else as my life's companion." Would it be easy for him to come and live here, in this village? Was he making this sacrifice, for my sake? I began to feel a little uneasy. His renunciation – would it become my burden? It frightened me. Once again I ran my eyes over the lines.

"My dearest"

I laughed. I had got used to looking at everything with fear and hesitation. The fact was that he had given in to me, and that was not just a victory, it proved and reinforced my independence. I put the letter carefully back into its cover. By the time I had locked the room and the clinic there was a steadiness in my step. This letter was going to change my life. I must be prepared for this change.

Suddenly I thought of Appa. How he received this piece of

news would not be a problem, I knew he wouldn't have any objection at all. Yet, the bond between Appa and me – would it grow stronger or weaker with Shiva's arrival?

The question shook me, just a little.

Seven

Walking back to the house, it seemed to me that the whole world had changed in the space of an hour. The grass on the lawn looked greener than it had before. The hibiscus running wild at one end of the compound had sprouted a great profusion of flowers, many more than I remembered having noticed earlier. My self-esteem had risen to a lofty eminence. I felt like an empress reigning over the whole wide earth… Like rajas and ranis in the movies who take off their fake pearl necklaces and grandly bestow them on supplicants, I was in a mood to slip off whatever jewellery I wore on my neck and wrists and present it to the first person who approached me for any help. Such was the inordinate benevolence bubbling up in my breast. Compassion!

"Compassion won't spring up at all in a life without passion! That's a life full of frustration and disappointment!" That's what Kamalini had once told me . Nobody had ever passionately loved Kali, she said. That was why she had stuck out her tongue and set off to destroy the demons. No religion had female goddesses like there were in the Hindu pantheon, she said. If all women had turned into Kalis, our men wouldn't have been able to stand it, she said. So they created a character like Sita – to jump into the fire when somebody said, "Jump!" To leave at once when somebody said, "Get out of the house!' For somebody to say to her: "This is exactly what will happen to you if you cross over any line that's laid down by a man!"

It occurred to me that I could now describe myself as a victorious Kali. Victorious in love. I was a Kali in love. Pidaari, that's what Paati used to call me whenever I had a temper tantrum. A fearsome female – cohort of the goddess or Bhadrakali herself.

A doubt assailed me: if Paati were alive would she have approved of my love? Would she have given her consent? For people of our caste, wealth and money are the only acceptable way to measure the worth of any man. Disregarding those indicators and just going and falling in love, and actually fixing up a husband for oneself was an indecent thing to do. Obscene! All these people, including Paati, belonged to a generation which continued to nurture a moral code dating from Victorian times, despite squirming uncomfortably under it. If I were to announce, "I like a certain man, I wish to marry him," for people of that generation what it means is, "I am lusting after this man, I want to go to bed with him." For women who have always lived and learned to be satisfied in a confined space, friendship and sharing are words which remain stunted; words whose potential will never be delineated. And when those ideas are allowed to expand and yield their full meaning, they cause bewilderment and panic. There is the fear that if you emerge from within the boundaries and step into the outside world, you'll be laughed at in the open bazaar.

How far I've travelled from Paati's curtailed existence!

"I accept your conditions." To me, this felt like an unbelievable victory. That is, he was ready and willing to come and live with me.

"If any fellow comes to you like that, he's after your wealth and property! A fat good-for-nothing, fit only to gobble free food!" The memory of Kamalini's words made me laugh. In her eyes no man had any character. I must tell her: "The man who has consented to marry me is not coming because he wants my property! He wants me! He desires me, for my own sake!"

Up until now Shiva had never asked me for anything. I doubted he knew anything of my background. Kamalini would not support the arrangement we were making. She would tell me it was wrong to expect such a sacrifice from a man who had a fine future before him, all on account of my stubborn insistence that he come and live with me, rather than the other way round. But I had absolutely no feeling of guilt. Maybe my stubbornness had forced his hand, but I wasn't to blame for it. It was like Amma making herself utterly indispensable to Appa. Only I had used no wiles at all to achieve my victory.

"Vanakkam,'kka!"

I looked up, startled. Wincing in the piercing noonday sunlight, my eyes made out a woman standing by the clinic gate. She was obviously waiting to see me. A familiar face. Suddenly I remembered her. She was the widow from Belukurichi who had turned up with a septic abortion. Again?

Glancing doubtfully at her, I said, "What, amma? On Sundays I see only urgent cases."

"I have not come for that, `nga, akka!" she said, with her head lowered.

"Then what is the matter?"

"Give me work, akka, any kind of work! Enough for *kanji* or *koozh* only. I'll drink it and just curl up in corner here, please!" Before she could finish, she was all choked up with misery, and her eyes were brimming. It looked like she had come on her own.

"You are from Belukurichi, right?"

"Yes, `nga. I have run away without telling anyone."

She seemed greatly distraught, her lips quivering as she spoke. There was a trembling in her fingers.

"Come in, come and talk inside. What is this, amma, coming suddenly and saying give me a job? How?" I muttered and sat down on the low wall of the clinic verandah.

"I came thinking you will help me, `nga, akka." The tears began again. My mind, which had dressed itself up in wings and taken flight just a few minutes earlier, now sat itself wearily down, dragged cruelly back to the real world.

"But I don't even know who you are, amma. What's your name?"

"Akila." She raised her head and gave me an unexpectedly steady look. "I am a woman. Apart from that, how can I identify myself, akka?"

Amazing, I thought. What a sophisticated argument she's using! Outsmarting me!

"Brothers or sisters, father and mother — Don't you have anyone?

""They're all there. They don't have the means to keep me and feed me. It's a year since my husband died. I am in my mother-in-law's house. I cannot describe what I have to endure there!" Her face flushed with rage. I sat quiet and let her speak.

"All day long I am a servant. At night they say I must go to any of the brothers who calls me, `kka!" She covered her face with her sari edge and sobbed. "I feel like hanging myself. But I don't have the courage, akka!"

I had no doubt that she was telling the truth. She couldn't have been more than twenty-five, and she was good-looking. Abruptly I recalled Draupadi of the *Mahabharatha*. Thinking it was Arjuna she had espoused, what did she do when she found that she had to sleep with four other men as well?

"But there is no work for you here, amma, what can I do? Why don't you go home now, I'll send for you in the morning."

Instantly she sat down on the ground and clasped my feet tightly. "Don't send me away, akka. If you don't give me a place to stay, there is no way out for me except to die."

In a flash, I lost my temper. The compassion that had bubbled up in me a little while ago, was maya. Illusion. It had come out of a feeling of self-satisfaction. Besides, this woman is a caricature, a symbol of sheer defeatism. They way I am now, I don't wish to acknowledge the slightest trace of failure.

"Do you think I'm running a home for orphans here? If your mother-in-law's house is not good enough go to your own family! Won't the parents who gave you birth understand? Work hard, and keep yourself alive!"

But she just stood there, weeping. It burned me up that she had utterly ruined my mood. Appa would be waiting for me for lunch. I had planned to speak to him persuasively about Shiva's letter. I felt furious that this woman had wrecked it all.

"Look here, just leave them! Are you living there just because you get food and shelter? You're a single woman, what's the problem with earning and supporting yourself? Do you have children?"

"No, `nga."

"Then why stay there?" She stood there without answering. Then she asked, slowly.

"Can't I get a job here, akka?"

"If you turn up and ask me, like this, out of the blue, where can I find a job for you?

"I will do anything, akka."

"Every single slot is occupied here. Come after ten days. I'll talk to someone and see what I can do." I got up. She had no choice but to leave.

But what was it that had given her hope, and brought her running here? It bothered me.

Shutting the clinic gate behind me, I hurried home. Raasamma was waiting at the door. "What, akka? Was there a case, or something? Appa is waiting for you for lunch."

I went in quickly. Appa was sitting in the hall watching TV.

"Come, Appa, let's eat," I said. "I went to get something from the clinic. An old patient came there and just sat."

A Bengali film was running on TV. Appa switched it off and got up. "What work did you have at the clinic?" he said casually.

"There was a letter I had forgotten, so I went to fetch it."

Appa did not ask me about the letter. These days he didn't talk much. I didn't ask him who finally lit the pyre in Pandurangan's house, and he didn't tell me.

He knows what subjects will get me all worked up, and he's avoiding them. But I am conscious of being made vulnerable by his silence. I don't have the energy to pierce through his thought processes. It seems to me that my greatest weakness, even now, is that I've become used to holding myself to blame for whatever disappointments he harbours in his mind.

"Are you going out anywhere today, Appa?" I asked.

"No, amma. I will go for a walk in the evening, as usual. Why do you ask?"

"I have to talk to you about something."

Appa smiled. "Oho! Why the preamble?"

Raasamma butted in, fussily offering, "Some poriyal, akka?"

"Something important," I said in English.

With a tilt of his head, Appa indicated his assent. "Because you came late, I have already taken my nap. After you finish eating, come upstairs," he said.

After fussing some more, asking me if I wanted this and wanted that, Raasamma finally switched on the TV and sat down. The Bengali movie was still going on.

"You say you can't understand the Tamil in the *Mahabharatha*. Can you understand this, Raasamma?" I said, laughing.

"It's some kind of love story, akka. That I can understand, whatever the language."

I chuckled. The annoyance I had felt a little earlier disappeared, and in its place came a feeling of exhilaration. Raasamma was joyfully watching the Bengali lovers. The saint Jnanasambandar grew ecstatic at the sight of the divine pair, Isan and Uma. There must be the same kind of Freudian explanation for both these ecstasies, I thought.

I followed Appa upstairs. He sat down in his easy-chair and calmly asked, "Who was the letter from, amma?"

Feeling faintly surprised, I smiled. "So you understood that I was coming to speak to you about the letter?"

"Two is added to two to make four. What is so strange about that?"

"Not bad!" I praised. "It looks like I underestimated you!"

"I can even guess who wrote the letter."

"Who?" I asked, in astonishment.

"Doctor Shivakumar."

"Oh! Has he written to you also?"

"Yes."

All of a sudden I felt bashful. And thankful that Shiva had so wisely managed to make things easier for me.

"What has he written?"

"Why don't you read it yourself and see?" he said, trying to rise, but I stopped him.

"No, Just tell me, that will be enough."

"I don't understand any of this 'love' and so on and so forth. Seems he has 'loved' you for five years. There was mention of some boy, once before – is this him?" asked Appa.

"Yes.'

"He says you were very obstinate all these years."

"Even now."

"What about?"

"Hasn't he written about that?"

"No. He probably thinks I know about it."

A hurt feeling came through in his tone of voice.

I said, "If he wants to marry me, I have told him he must come to this town, and live in this house with me. That's my condition."

Appa's face suddenly looked quite different. I went on, "He didn't agree all these years. Now he has agreed."

"For what reason?"

"He says he can't live without me! So, the gentleman has given up his principles, all for the sake of Love!" I laughed.

Appa didn't laugh. He sat there, looking thoughtful.

"Do you think that it is the truth?"

Taken aback, I exclaimed, "I think it's true! Why, do you have any doubt about it?"

"The whole thing seems absurd to me. That `condition' of yours seems absurd, and him saying he'll come here – *that* also sounds absurd to me!"

"Absurd? How do you mean?"

"Just take his situation, to start with. He has a good practice in Hyderabad. He is used to living in comfort in a big city. Why should he agree to come here, to this village?"

I giggled. "That's Love! Are you telling me you don't understand that?"

It was then that I noticed that there was not the slightest trace of laughter in his face.

"All right," he said. "Let that go. Where is the need for him to come here?"

"My condition! I told you that was the condition I laid down!"

"That's what I'm asking you – what was that for? Did I ever tell you I wanted a *maapillai* who would live in this house?"

There was a feeling of slipping...sliding. Like a train going off the rails.

"You didn't tell me. I said it myself, and I am saying it now as well. I do not wish to leave this house."

Appa sat there without speaking, looking stricken and perplexed about how he must respond to this. Then he rose slowly, went to the window and gazed interestedly at whatever was going on outside. Unexpectedly I felt distraught. It made me very unhappy that Appa was surprised at such a small thing.

"I don't wish ever to leave you, "I said. "After Amma died it was my responsibility to take care of you." Appa suddenly swung around and faced me.

"Just for that, compelling an outsider to come and live here? What sort of justice is that?"

"But I didn't compel him! 'If you wish to come, come!' I told him. 'Otherwise, we can put an end to our relationship.'"

For a little while Appa said nothing. Then he spoke as though he were measuring out the words very carefully. "There is one thing you have forgotten. This is my house. A person about whom nothing is known, nothing about what he is, or what he's going to be —to bring such a man to live in this house, without my permission—how can you arrive at such a decision all by yourself?'

The words fell like whiplashes. My mouth could not open at all. Speech had got utterly stopped up in me. I felt amazed that it had never dawned on me that such a question could ever be asked.

The letter which I had thought was my triumphant prize lay forlorn in my palm.

Eight

"This is my house."

Eyes shut, or eyes open, the words rose up in front of me in gigantic shapes. I turned over and lay with my face pressed into the pillow. They crept in through my eyelids.

"*This is my house.*" From the sloping-roofed verandahs in front to the first of the four halls of the long, old fashioned house, all the way to the fourth where Raasamma lived, the words unrolled like a curl of video film. As the east, the west, the north and the south revolved one after the other, the words flaunted all their angles like a mocking camera. And everywhere I turned there stood Appa, filling the space between floor and ceiling, and from the walls around echoed his words: "*This is my house.*" As though he were saying: "There isn't the smallest corner for you here." I cringed from the soles of my feet to the roots of my hair.

I remembered when I was little Amma told me a story about a crow and a sparrow. When the crow opened the door, the silly sparrow waiting outside thought it was being offered shelter from the rain. "So you're cold, are you?" asked the crow. "Come lie on this dosai-pan, it'll feel so nice and warm!" The cruel words came back to me. There was no difference between the sparrow's predicament and mine today, I thought. How clever I had thought myself, taking my proposition to Appa, and having Appa fling it back at me, like a dosai-pan!

"This is my house.... Without my permission, how could you come to this decision all by yourself?"

From the standpoint of logic, it was a perfectly fair question. On the assumption that the bond between us transcended logic, I had made a stupid calculation, and it had gone wrong. Because I was born female, I could never become a permanent member of this household, I just didn't have the right. A son-in-law with unknown antecedents and prospects could not be accepted, the way a daughter-in-law with unknown antecedents and prospects could. If you asked why not, well, it was a question of dominance.

There was a soft rap at the door, and Raasamma's voice calling out, "Akka, Akka." I did not answer. I lay there with my eyes closed. I knew why she was calling. The women from our farmlands had arrived to perform their 'kummi' dance. After the festival of Pongal, they always came to sing us their rain-songs and be given rice and bananas in return. It was a ritual, year after year – their gathering in the outer courtyard to raise a song of prayer to Varuna, the Rain God. Even if each voice dragged the *raga* along in a different direction, they had the rhythm down pat, and always clapped their hands without missing a beat.

My window overlooked the courtyard.

"Akka hasn't got up at all, Ayya" Raasamma was saying to Appa.

"She's lying down with a headache, don't bother her. Let them do their dance and go," he told her.

"*Thaney, thaney*!" sang one of the women, beginning with the refrain. Four or five voices could be heard joining in

Oh. King of the skies, come down as rain, holy one!
Without rice to eat, we field-women waste away
Bring down black columns of rain, Lean on the earth with your dark legs.
(Thaney, thaney!)
Yet why isn't it turning dark at all?
Oh, why won't the sacred rain fall?
Won't the clouds lean on those slopes
And come down in a flood?

(Thaney, thaney!)
We stirred up a potful of flour-paste
And drew many kolams in the marketplace
Oh won't a million droplets fall
To wash away the kolams we made?
(Thaney, thaney!)

With my eyes closed I could see the women singing and dancing in a circle. I knew each of them – Anjalai, Karuppi, Saroja, Rukkumini, Neelamma – they would have bathed, and with cheeks gleaming gold with turmeric paste and saris pleated at the back and tucked in tight, they would be in high spirits, talking and laughing. As they began to sing and clap the kummi, the high spirits would vanish. Absorbed in the words of the song, or maybe out of worry that they might forget the words, their faces would grow tense.

"Now, supposing we have just sung in ten houses, by the time we reach the eleventh it will start raining." Anjalai had told me.

"I will write about this to the government," I had replied, in jest.

"It is true, Amma!" They were offended.

Nobody had put it to the test, but Anjalai laid down a condition: "You do it with faith, and definitely there will be a good result!"

For no reason at all tears formed in my eyes and pushed their way through my closed lids. Every year it was I who offered *vetrilai-paaku,* the hospitality gift to them, along with rice and money, in the belief that I was honouring those who came to my house. Anjalai didn't know that groundless beliefs do not have good results.

The sounds downstairs had ceased. Each woman spoke a few humble words in parting, and made her departure. That not one of them said, "Let the young mistress come and give us our presents!" was a keen disappointment. How affectionate these women were to my face! How many of them had I delivered of their children! How many have had unwanted children aborted by me! Had they forgotten everything and just gone off, once their sari pallus were filled with rice and money?

All of a sudden I felt defenceless. A feeling of weakness seized me. On a certain twilight evening the colour of ashes, in a courtyard imprinted with black shadows my mother had sat, utterly distraught, and it was that same mood of hers which now assailed me. I understood how terrible the shock she suffered then must have been – how much more terrible than the one I had just received. Because she had somehow lived through that calamity, Appa must have consoled himself with the belief that she had come through it whole. But I knew she had not come through. I could not explain to anybody my distress at not being able to solve the riddle she had set me. I couldn't clarify why I felt compelled to drag along that burden of distress. That was why I couldn't answer that question of his:

How can you – without my permission, and all by yourself – arrive at any decision?

The question completely unsettled me. I stood there for some seconds as though my brain had gone inert, my eyes staring from their sockets.

It seemed to me that there had been more anger than despair in Appa's face. Why this anger? Was it at the thought of my foolishness? By deciding on my own that I was his direct heir, and thus also an owner of this house, had I made things awkward for him? Was it presumptuous of me to try and establish that I was just as good as a son? It felt as though he were asking, "*Your* house? Who told you that?" In that instant I realized that I had assumed too much. I felt miserable at the thought of all the effort I had put into it, and into waiting for the outcome. I hung my head. Determined not to let tears appear in my eyes, I pulled myself together.

"Oh! I hadn't thought of it from that angle. Of course, it was a mistake," I said. Wearily I rose, smiling. "If you don't care for this arrangement, I don't want to get married. You and this house are what are important to me."

Before Appa could say anything I had left the room and gone into my own room and locked myself in. Now, when I think back, the words I spoke sounded as if they belonged in a film script. Really there was no great difference between Raasamma and myself. Just as she had sacrificed her youth, when the elders in her family decided that she should not marry a second time, out of a desire to avoid conflict, I was saying, "This house is what matters to me!" That was the screen of illusion that I drew across my own vision, as I crushed in my palm the unexpected chance at life that had come within my grasp. As I flung it away.

Entering my room, I opened my palm. Shiva's letter lay crushed there, the words crumpled and pulled out of shape by perspiration. Crushing it further into a tight ball, I flung it into the wastepaper basket.

I had no idea what impact my words had had on Appa. He was not opposing my marriage. What he was saying was: "Afterwards, get out!" He was saying, "Go to your husband's house, that's the proper thing to do. As his wife, you will become one of his family. There'll be no need for you to hang on here. This is the patriarchal tradition. Don't you try to change it!"

I will change it. Traditions must be broken.

The folly of searching for somebody to light the funeral pyre, when your own daughter was there – that must never happen here, the way it did for Pandurangan just because nobody thought it possible to challenge the belief of the villagers.

If a boy had been born instead of me, I don't think anybody would have taken care of you like this, from the crack of dawn to when you go to sleep at night. "Have you eaten? Have you slept? Would you like a thuvaiyal, *do you want chapatis, shall I check your blood pressure, has your veshti come back from the laundry?" Nobody would have cared for you like that. I'm not saying I did all this because I am myself. Any girl in my place would have done as much. That's just what you haven't understood. That Pandurangan's daughter would have done as much. I know the anguish she must have felt, when she was told she was not good enough to light the funeral pyre.*

Time crept on. My obstinacy hardened. My thoughts refused to budge. It was as though glue had spread over them.

If you expect me to leave after I get married, then I don't want such a marriage. I'll think it a dream that the letter ever came. A dream that gave me an hour of happiness.

This war of mine will go on. Until you say to me, "This is your house." Until then, let my youth be spent hovering about here like a disconsolate spirit. Burdened with this penance, as an ascetic is burdened with his saffron bundle. Never mind. There will be so many outlets for frustration. And I possess the will to construct them for myself. But remaining here is my birthright, whether you want it or not.

Shiva? What would Shiva think? He would be angry, that was certain. "This is a gone case," he would come to realize, soon enough. My heart felt heavy. I got up.

Outside the window was an encircling darkness. It did not occur to me to put on the light in the room, so oblivious was I to the darkness, so absorbed in my thoughts. I had never been like this before. I felt ashamed at the way I was cowering, like a defeated woman. Switching on the table lamp, I went to the bathroom and washed my face, splashing water on it. The face that looked back at me looked dead. Hurriedly, I came out of the room.

The TV was on in the hall. And Raasamma was nowhere to be seen. Just as irritation crackled up in me, I heard her voice at the door.

"Take her somewhere else, Ayya. Amma is not well, she's been lying down the whole day."

Indistinct voices sounded from outside.

"Are there no other doctors in this town or what? You should go there without wasting any more time – Amma is not well, don't you understand?"

In a couple of strides I was at the door. A horse-drawn carriage stood there and a man and a woman were standing at the gate.

"What is it, Raasamma?" I asked.

Raasamma turned around with a jerk. "You've got up, `mma?" she asked, sounding relieved. "Some urgent case, amma. They're standing there insisting that you, and you alone, must attend to it."

I went to the gate. The woman looked middle-aged.

"Who is it, amma? Who is ill, and what's the illness?"

"Thayee, only you can save us!" she said, with tears in her eyes. "Daughter's lying there dying." She pointed to the wagon. The man standing by didn't open his mouth.

"You're bringing her when she's about to die? What is the illness?" I said, with some annoyance.

"Only you must look at her and say that, thayee," she said, with a sob. "Already my daughter has come to you before this."

I didn't understand. It was dark inside the carriage. A female shape lay curled up, unconscious.

"Bring the carriage to the clinic." I told them.

"I'll go and open up, akka," Raasamma said, and ran ahead.

As I sat there in the examination room, the man carried the girl in as though she were a young goat and laid her on the table. It gave me a shock. It was the girl who had come that afternoon, that Akila, who had begged, "Can I get work here?" She who had threatened, "If you don't give me work I will have to hang myself."

"Wretch!' I cursed, and hurried to the table. "What happened to her?" I lifted her wrist and felt her pulse.

She was dead.

"She ate bug poison, amma!" said the mother.

"Why?"

"It is my fate, thayee! Her in-laws' place was not good. And in her own family I am useless. I myself am dependent on my daughter-in-law. She was not allowed to stay. Let her live and she and I will do coolie work. Drink our kanji together."

"You should have thought of this before," I said wearily. "Now it's no use. Your daughter is dead."

"Dead? Oh, you wicked fool!" Rushing forward, she raised a screech like a wounded bird. The son waiting outside came in. The woman struck herself on the belly and on the mouth.

"You told her she couldn't stay in the house where she was born, you chased her out! So she has gone, the blessed one. She didn't want your mercy."

He stood there as though very shocked, himself. Then, without saying a word he gathered her up and walked out. She who had given birth to the dead girl followed him, weeping and wailing.

"I am going, thayee," she said, and then, as though suddenly remembering something. "She used to say she was going to ask you for work, the wretched thing. Oh, she's gone like a mad creature!"

Her wailing remained audible for quite some time, even after the horse-carriage had left.

"Did that girl die, akka?"

It was then I noticed that Raasamma was still standing there.

My body trembled a little. It sounded to me as though she — was saying, "You are the one who is responsible for this."

"Why did she die?"

"Raasamma, I don't know," I replied, tired. "On the whole, it must have been because she didn't have the courage to live, isn't it, that she died?"

Raasamma, who was walking in front, beaming the flashlight on the path, turned abruptly at this: "What could she live for? No education, no husband, no support in the house where she was born, no support in the house which she entered when she got married. Day after day she was dying, so she must have felt why not die once and for all?"

"Did you know her?"

"I didn't know her. Her mother was standing outside and crying about it."

What Akila had told me came to mind: "Apart from just being a woman, how else can I identify myself, akka?" Raasamma had perceived that identity much more clearly than I had, it seemed.

"Dying is no solution, Raasamma. If women are ready to die, society is just waiting to kill them off," I told her, with sudden earnestness.

"You are talking like Krishna does on TV!" Raasamma said, and laughed.

Nine

"How many more, Meenatchi?" I asked. Meenatchi opened the door slightly and peeped out. "Twenty, twenty-five people there'll be," she replied. "Why,'ka? Do you have to go out somewhere?"

"No," I said, shaking my head. Twelve o'clock. If there were twenty-five patients, I'd need at least three hours more. "Tell Raasamma that there are many more patients waiting. Appa need not wait for me for lunch. Tell her to send my food here."

"Why,`kka? Why not tell these people to wait for half an hour? In the meantime you can go and have your lunch and come."

I felt a quick sting of anger. I snapped at her, "Just do what I tell you, Meenatchi!"

She stared, taken aback. Then she said, "All right. I'll tell Paavaayee to go and tell her," and left.

The girl huddled on my stool was squirming like a mouse. It was her first delivery, and already her face had gone white with fear and helplessness. My grim expression was obviously causing her further consternation. As I examined her, I scolded, "Why do you wear your skirt and bra so tight?" To her mother standing on the other side of the screen I said threateningly, "If you dose her with castor oil or anything like that, I won't attend to her delivery!" Today I felt like spitting out my rage at everybody. I felt no sensitivity, no guilt on that account, either.

My mentor, Dr Lakshmi, suddenly came to mind. A doctor acclaimed for her magical healing touch, it was from her that I received my training when I was a house-surgeon. There was never any talk of even a single case of hers turning out badly. However, not even for therapeutic purposes did that lady ever wear a smile on her face. Did she have any human feeling? I doubted it. If a woman cried out in childbirth, she would retort, "*Chhee*! Shut up! When you went with your husband you enjoyed it, didn't you?" The curses she came out with were even cruder. Many were the days when I recoiled with disgust at the way she talked. We would cite psychological reasons for such behaviour and satisfy ourselves. The poor woman had been defeated in love. Her parents had not approved of her romance. Her feeling of being thwarted had turned to poison, poised to drip from the tip of her tongue.

The thought that I might turn out to be Dr Lakshmi's spiritual heir not only didn't shock me, it even made me feel a kind of pride. Perceiving my mood but without understanding the cause, Meenatchi kept her mouth shut as she jotted down notes about each patient and sent them in to me, one by one. Ordinarily, I had every patient's entire history down by heart, they used to vomit it all out to me as if I were a psychiatrist. Today I was not in a condition to take on all their burdens. I functioned mechanically, without talking, almost as though I had been possessed of by Dr Lakshmi's soul.

Souls wander about, it seems, yearning for human bodies to inhabit. When they find weak persons, they swoop down and nab them, they say. I had laughed, when someone who believed in the spirit world told me this. Now, as I thought about Dr Lakshmi I felt I had been transformed in like manner, and it disturbed me. There was a rumour that Dr Lakshmi had committed suicide. Mangamma, Lakshmi, that Akila who had died yesterday, as vaporous effusions all their frustrations and oppressions, all their griefs and furies would seize and convulse me.

As a child, when I went with Paati to a Mariamman temple, I remember seeing a woman standing there, her hair in disarray, breathing stertorously, her head jerking like a Thanjavur doll, her body twitching. The pujari was in a terrible temper. He was speaking to her in strange words, and hitting her with a bunch of neem leaves. The crowd around seemed to be watching appreciatively. Terrified, I buried my face in Paati's sari pleats and began to cry. My whimpering, "Let's go! Let's go!" prompted Paati to lift me up and take me to the carriage we had come in. As we drove back I buried my face in her lap again, moaning, "Why, why are they beating her?"

"A ghost must have caught hold of that girl, so the pujari is beating it to send it away," said Paati matter-of-factly,

"What does that mean?"

Paati did not answer my question properly. She said, "Some ill wind, or some black thing must have touched her. That's why they say that a girl who has come of age shouldn't go out alone."

Paati's words disturbed me even more. "Why should ghosts only catch hold of girls?" I asked. By that time Paati had lost interest. "That's just the way it is. There's the proverb, isn't there? That if a girl who's come of age goes out, even ghosts will turn up to catch hold of her. Now keep quiet and stop bothering me."

For several days the memory of that wild-haired woman tormented me. It was only after I had obtained my doctor's degree and started the clinic that I grasped the meaning of the proverb. It struck me that for the women who came here, it was I who was the pujari. It was my task to drive out the ghosts inhabiting their bodies.

Right now, though, it looked like I needed a pujari myself. Meenatchi came and informed me that four women were waiting for scans to be done. Making them drink water, and keeping them from going to the lavatory to pass urine was her task, and she found it a highly demanding one.

I got up. On the bench outside sat the pregnant women, squirming uncomfortably. Shameless women, I cursed inwardly, and went into the scan room. None of them had any problem with the pregnancy, they had come just to find out if the foetus was male or female. Today, it so happened that all four of them had female foetuses. Without so much as wincing at the thought, each had come prepared to have her daughter aborted.

As a female foetus, its face bowed, displayed its buttocks on the screen, the memory of the pujari suddenly came to me. "Go away! Go away! How brazen you are to turn up here!" he shouted, as he struck. Distraught, I switched off the screen.

Knowing how to enter was no problem, the problem was how to exit. Irrelevantly Abhimanyu came to mind. He knew how to break into the *chakravyuh*, the strategic maze formation of the Kaurava army. But he had no idea how to exit. Dronacharya had watched impotently as the Kaurava hordes thrust aside the laws of warfare and cut him to pieces. A strange feeling came over me — that I was at once both Abhimanyu and Dronacharya.

It was four in the evening by the time I managed to finish all the work. Appa would have gone out. His was an extensive trading empire, but he had never told me about it in any detail. Today the reasons for his not telling me were becoming clear to me—he just did not want me to know, he didn't want any future husband of mine to know. He was afraid that any son-in-law who consented to come and live in this house would find out all about it. I was certain that his anxiety stemmed from his inability to accept me as his rightful heir.

In a flash a question came up in my mind. Was he searching for a male heir? Could he be planning to adopt someone, as some people we knew in the villages around had done? Is that why he felt a son-in-law living in the house would be a hindrance? Adoption would be convenient for him for several reasons. Hunting for some fellow or other to dispose of him, as had happened to Pandurangan, wouldn't be necessary. If he were making arrangements for an adoption without my knowledge, as he had done earlier for a second marriage, I could do nothing about it. I did not even have the protection of the law. I was suddenly acutely conscious of my vulnerable position. I had been present to argue for amma's sake, to cite moral reasons, but there was no one to argue for me, and it frightened me. That Abhimanyu who was trapped in a *chakravyuh* —really he was none other than me! I pitied myself. It seemed to me that it was an injustice that had begun when I was still in the womb.

As I came out of the room, Paavaayee, Meenatchi and Muniappan were all whispering together about something. Meenatchi shrank back, aware, as she was, of my frame of mind that day.

"What are you all talking about?" I asked, a little defensively.

"Nothing at all, `mma," Paavaayee replied, with a friendly smile. "Yesterday that Belukurichi girl's mother brought her as a dead body, it seems, and asked you to save her. We were talking about that."

I started. What she was saying meant something new, it seemed to me.

"What about it?"

"Did that woman say the girl herself ate the bug poison, amma?"

"Yes, what about it?"

"They are saying her own brother killed her."

What was this — a new story?

"Who?"

"In Thottiyapatti. That girl's native place. This morning some people we know came from there. 'Paavaayee!' they said to me. `Look what is happening! Even if you are born together and have the same blood, your stomachs are different!' they said again and again, they were so upset."

Casting my mind back, I recalled the shock on the youth's face when I told him that Akila had died.

"People may be spreading these tales, but I refuse to believe them," I said sternly. "Couldn't it have been suicide?"

"It could have been, of course. But the whole town is talking. The police have also been asking questions. They will come to see you also, 'nga."

An unnecessary headache, I thought, with annoyance. "We'll see about that when it happens. You go and do your work, each of you," I told them, and set off for the house. For a while a nagging feeling of guilt kept pricking at me inside. I felt angry with Akila for having put me in such a position. What was Akila to me, anyway? Was there some bond or identity that we shared, from a previous birth?

"*I am a woman. Apart from that, how can I identify myself?*" She had confounded me with the question. It was that which bound us together, and my lacking the courage to accept it was what was making me feel guilty. Telling myself that anybody in my position would have done the same thing, I forced myself to break free of this thought.

When I reached home, Appa's car was not to be seen. That calmed me a little. After yesterday's argument, I hadn't spoken to him, I hadn't even seen him. Nor had he come looking for me. Maybe he thought the matter had been settled. Just to make it clear to him that it was not all over, I clung to my vow of silence.

There was Kamalini, seated in the central hall. Why had she turned up now, without letting me know she was coming? As the question occurred to me, I realized I was in no mood to meet her.

"Oh, hello. What's this, your majesty has suddenly come to

call on us?" I remarked, pretending to be overjoyed.

As soon as she heard my voice she put down the book she was reading, enthusiastically embraced me and kissed me on the cheek. The short hairstyle had now been transformed into a close crop.

"Yes, it's very sudden. I came to Coimbatore, had an extra day, and thought I would just come and see you. I'm leaving tomorrow evening."

I gave a dispirited smile. "What's the hurry?" I said, hospitably.

"This is all the time I have now," she said ingenuously. "Thought if I come and gossip a bit with you, it'll be relaxing."

"Madam came just now `nga," said Raasamma, entering with a tumbler of coffee. "I have started making tiffin. I'll bring it as soon as it is ready."

"Look around for a person like Raasamma for me, if you can!" said Kamalini.

"Why do you need a person?"

"Because the person I am going to marry doesn't know how to cook!" she said, laughing.

"Marry! What's this, a joke?" I said, astonished.

"Why, can't I get married?"

"Go right ahead. But does that fellow know you well?"

"Every inch, he knows every inch," she said, laughing again.

"And what about all those declarations? Your opinions? Your philosophy?"

"He knows. Yet he says he will marry me. Isn't that funny?"

"Very funny," I said, chuckling. "Who is this great soul?"

"He's got a business. Hasn't studied a lot. But he's a good person. No hypocrisy in him. I am fed up of all the hypocrites around me. I am tired of all these debates about science, there's no warmth in them. He won't stand in the way of my activities, he won't be jealous of me. Seems to me he'll be my friend. I don't know what he sees in me. He asked, will you marry me? That day the question sounded absurd to me. But when I thought about it, I felt that among all the men I know he's the most straightforward. And I said yes."

That an ardent feminist like her had so easily found a way out made me envious. "I'm amazed, Kamalini!"

"Yes, it *is* amazing," said Kamalini, "What about you? You said you would marry only someone who would live here, did you find anybody?"

I did not want to say anything within earshot of Raasamma. "Come, let's go upstairs. We'll sit in my room and talk." We'd just reached when the telephone rang. Quickly returning downstairs in a few bounds, I told Raasamma, "If anybody phones from Hyderabad and asks for me, tell them I have gone out on a case. Tell them I will phone when I come back." By the time she had picked up the receiver and started speaking, I was back upstairs. I readied myself to continue telling Kamalini the story of my love-life which had ended with the very first chapter.

Raasamma was hurrying up the stairs. I waited for her to come, and then leave quickly.

Ten

Raasamma arrived and stood, panting. "Akka, Akka…" she stuttered, confusedly. I was afraid he was going to blurt out something in front of Kamalini.

"I'm just coming, Kamalini," I said and hurried towards Raasamma, at the door. Asking "What is it, Raasamma?" I nudged her towards the upstairs verandah. "Who phoned?" Certain it must have been Shiva, I felt my face flushing.

Raasamma looked strange, panic spreading over her face.

"Ayya is in the big hospital in Salem, it seems. And the police have come! They are standing outside."

Jolted, I cried, "Hospital? Who says? What do the police have to do with it? Tell me properly, Raasamma!"

"But I don't know, `mma! They have come, and they are standing there saying they want to see you!"

I remembered, suddenly. They must have come to make enquiries about Akila.

"Tell them to wait a bit. Who told you about Appa?"

"It's Maanikkam. He is waiting on the phone for you."

"Fool!" I shouted at her. "Why didn't you tell me this right away?" I ran downstairs two steps at a time, and by the time I picked up the phone my chest was bursting. Sweat had broken out on my brow.

"This is Maanikkam speaking, `nga." His voice was agitated.

"Where're you speaking from? Did you say Appa isn't well? What happened suddenly? When did you go to Salem?"

"At eleven o'clock this morning we came here on work, `kka. He ate, rested, and came out at four o'clock to come back, and all of a sudden he had chest pain and sat down on the steps. The ayya who was with him admitted him in a nursing home."

"Which nursing home?" As Maanikkam spoke, I hurriedly noted it down.

"How is Appa now?" My throat had gone completely dry. Not words, but mere gusts of air seemed to be emerging from it.

"He is so-so," Manikkam's voice was husky. "They have inserted so many tubes. I don't know how to say it, `nga, `kka."

"I am coming right away. Tell Appa. Give him courage." Since my throat was getting stopped up and it was impossible for me to go on speaking, I thought I was the one who needed someone to give me courage.

"All right,`nga,'ka. Are you going to drive the car all by yourself at night-time?"

"I'm coming, stop worrying."

As I put the phone down, the thoughts and guilty feelings came in their hundreds and thousands, breaking over me in wave after wave. In this birth I would not be forgiven for having stayed away from Appa so stubbornly. For not having set eyes on him since yesterday. Right now, the traffic was very heavy. It would take an hour to reach Salem. I felt it was all a dream. As though I had been cut adrift.

"What is it, akka? How is Periayya?"

I turned towards Raasamma. She looked as if she'd burst into tears even before I gave her an answer.

"He is so-so. He's in a big hospital. A good one. I have to leave immediately, Raasamma."

"All alone?"

All at once my patience slid from me, making its escape. "How else?" I shouted. "Why do I need anybody to be with me? Are you saying I cannot manage this all alone, by myself?" Raasamma was quelled into silence. But then she said, wringing her hands, "But the police are waiting at the door!" Exhausted, I muttered "Oh God!" and hastened to the door. Two policemen stood there. One was a sub-inspector: I knew him.

"Vanakkam, 'mma," he said smiling.

"What is the matter, Perumaal?" I asked wearily. "My father has fallen ill and been admitted to the hospital in Salem. I have to leave urgently."

"All right then, `nga. We will come tomorrow and meet you. Just to ask you about that matter of the Thottiyapatti girl. Some say suicide, others say murder – even before the post-mortem was done, they tried to hush up the whole thing. They came to see you, it appears?"

"Yes, but she was already dead on arrival. I don't believe it is murder. It looks to me like suicide. Why, I gave them a note about it – what happened?"

"They never even reported it to the police, amma! We got the news and went there ourselves." I felt a quick, sharp prick of rage – was he daring to accuse me?

"How many cases we have seen like this, Perumaal! Has the habit of going to the police reached here, too? Tomorrow I shall come to the station and give a statement. Just leave me alone, now!"

Without even checking to see if they had left, I went quickly up the stairs, recalling that Kamalini was still sitting there. God, why so many problems today? I felt rattled. When that Akila turned up yesterday and begged, if only I had said, okay, I'll give you a job, if only I had said that word, she would not have committed suicide like this, and she wouldn't have brought me to such a state that the police came to ask questions! In the middle of my anxiety about Appa this thought gnawed at me. With uncomfortable aptness, a *kural* came to mind: "Greater than the entire universe is a small act of helpfulness, when given well in time."

"What's the matter, Mano? Is there a problem?" asked Kamalini.

"Yes. Appa went to Salem this morning, and there he got chest pain and he's been admitted to hospital. I have to leave for Salem right now."

"I'll come too."

"What for, Kamalini? You've only just arrived. Why don't you rest?"

"Nothing is wrong with me, Mano. In this kind of mental state you shouldn't be driving alone."

"Okay. Thank you," I said. The same thought must have occurred to Raasamma and Maanikkam and caused them to speak, I realized, and felt ashamed. Instead of importuning me to have tiffin, Raasamma had cleverly packed it in a basket and put it in the car. As I was about to leave, the telephone rang. "I'll see who it is, Akka," Raasamma sprang up like an arrow. I stood there, frozen, my legs hesitating to move. In a short while Raasamma returned. "That Hyderabad man spoke, Akka, I told him you had gone out of town."

I came to life. Shamelessly I asked, "Did he say anything else?"

"No, he said 'All right then' and put it down."

I started the car. Raasamma's warm hand touched my forearm. "Ayya will be all right, 'nga, 'kka, you don't worry. Drive carefully, 'nga, 'kka!"

As I nodded and smiled back at her, tears gathered in my eyes. A feeling of weakness crept into me: without these guardian deities whom I had installed around myself, would I have been able to accomplish anything on my own?

Until we had driven past all the narrow streets of the town and entered the highway, Kamalini did not say anything. Her silence was comforting. Today it seemed entirely probable that I might break down, under the sheer burden of my guilt. Like blind old Dhritarashtra, my mind tossed about from self-pity to self-hatred. I understood why he fulminated against Krishna, blaming him for having brought on the Mahabharata war. "When Arjuna said he would not make war, if Vasudevan had said, all right, you needn't, there wouldn't have been a war, and so many people wouldn't have died. Duryodhana wouldn't have felt compelled to slay Abhimanyu, and a vengeful Arjuna would not have gone in pursuit of my son-in-law, Jayadratha."

If Shiva's letter had not arrived, all these miseries wouldn't have occurred. Akila wouldn't have died, the police would not have come, and I would not have neglected Appa for a whole day and a half. My mind kept screaming, 'God! Oh God!' I agonized—if anything happened to Appa how will I ever be able to forgive myself?

Only I will light the pyre! Only I, only I will light it!

The memory of that frantic nightmare tormented me. Which ghoul had taken hold of me? Was it the spirit of Mangamma?

"Who is in Hyderabad?"

I was thrown off balance. Kamalini's presence, there, beside me, had completely slipped my mind. Should I tell her or not? I felt hesitant. I had never revealed myself fully to her, feeling that my way of looking at things and my burden of tradition and its absurdities would make no sense to her.

Yet, it was only to her that I could talk about the problem that had arisen because of Shiva.

"The man who has agreed to accept my condition and marry me."

Kamalini let out a faint whistle. "The chap who wants to live off you?"

I laughed. "No. He's a doctor with a practice in Hyderabad."

"Don't tell me!" Kamalini exclaimed in wonderment. "He says he'll come here?"

"Yes. He didn't agree easily. Kept postponing it for three years and now he's said yes."

"Why?"

"It's called Love. You wouldn't understand."

Kamalini focused her gaze on the road unwinding murkily ahead, and sank into thought. At last she murmured, "It's true – I don't get it. Do you love him?"

"Yes. But I can't say I'll die without him – it's not that sort of love."

"So, then what's the problem?"

"The problem is that my father doesn't want it. That is, he won't consent to the condition I've laid down. He's saying, how could I come to a decision without asking him?"

"Correct!" said Kamalini, ridiculously. "I'm on your father's side."

I sighed, resigned, and drove on. I wouldn't be able to explain anything to her. I just didn't have the vocabulary to tell her about the seed Amma had planted in me. To describe the ramifications of its growth, or to explain my compulsion to submit to its dictates. These were perceptions that had dissolved in my blood. They were impossible to capture in the filter of words. "I'm an uneducated woman, I don't know how to say it," Amma had said. An educated woman—that's what I was, and yet I couldn't articulate it either. Here I was, with my eyes blindfolded and obstinately setting out in search of some obscure goal. That is what it seemed like, even to me. Gandhari had blindfolded her eyes because she had the subtle vision which Dhritarashtra lacked. I wasn't Gandhari. Was I Dhritarashtra?

"What have you decided?"

"If Appa is not willing, I have decided I will never get married."

"Everything you say sounds absurd to me."

I did not answer. Appa had said the very same words to me.

Everything seemed absurd, with Appa in his present condition.

When I was not by his side, he had chest paid and had to be admitted to who knows what kind of hospital, and he now lay there like an orphan, without anyone to care for him. I felt sad that everything that I had intended to prove to him remained suspended, as it were, in mid-air.

"When I saw the letter he had written I really lost my balance, Kamalini. That day a girl came to the hospital gate and clung to my feet, crying, 'I'm in great trouble, give me some kind of job, or I'll have no other way but to die.' At that moment, showing the letter to my father appeared to me to be much more important. For no reason at all, I lost my temper with her. She went straight back and committed suicide, Kamalini! That night her mother turned up with the body. Now the police are also asking questions. Because I was so upset that night, I didn't insist on their going to the police at once."

"How did it happen?"

"It was all because of that letter. And Appa's reaction to it. I jumbled everything together and made a mess of it! Because we have influence with the local police, we'll manage somehow. But within me I feel disturbed that I have done wrong."

"Leave it be!" said Kamalini. "Right in the middle of this anxiety about Appa don't think of this now and get all confused. Did you ever imagine she would die, just because she said so?"

I felt somewhat comforted. On the horizon, there in the distance, lights appeared, a sign that we were approaching Salem. Except for thoughts about Appa, everything else slipped away once we entered the town. As I drove into the hospital compound, I caught sight of Maanikkam, standing on the steps. He ran towards us. I brought the car to a measured halt, my heart palpitating about what news he was going to give me.

"What is it, Maanikkam?"

"He is just the same, Akka. They are saying nobody should go to him. I.C. Unit, that is where he is, they say. Now that you have come, I have got back my life. Akka, only God knows what I have been through! Terrible!" Turning his face to hide the tears brimming in his eyes, Maanikkam wiped them off.

"I know how you must have suffered," I said gently, and calmed him. Then I hurried towards the I.C.U. Kamalini stood outside. Slipping off my chappals, I introduced myself to the nurse and went in. She reported that the doctor said it was a massive heart attack, and that the next twenty-four hours would be crucial. The duty doctor would be there in a short while, she said.

Appa lay with eyes closed on a hospital bed, with the upper part raised. The graph on the monitor near him leaped up and down. This was not the Appa I had seen day before yesterday. Not the man who had thrust out his chest and asserted, with such dignity: "This is my house!" Not the person who had demanded, "How dare you bring an outsider into this house without my permission?" This person lying here did not know how ridiculous his assertion was. This was the man who had sat down on the road like any destitute! This man was beyond demanding an explanation from any dog who dared to enter his house at will. Grief surged up and obscured my vision.

What did you think, when your chest hurt you? Were you frightened? Did you agonize that you had no son to run to your side? Did you think your fate would be identical to Pandurangan's?

With quivering fingers I felt his forehead.

I have been defeated. You know nothing about my defeat.

Appa's eyes opened. They blossomed in recognition.

"I suffered so much because you weren't nearby, Mano," he said.

Eleven

I cannot forget that look of Appa's. It felt as though arms were reaching out to me to bring me ashore just when I was on the point of drowning and the fear of death had gripped me by the throat. The radiance of that look touched to life every nerve, every muscle in me. At the time, Appa's arms knew no distinctions of gender. My feelings overpowered me, tears blurred my vision.

You thought of setting me apart, as one meant to go to another house. You attempted to direct my emotions elsewhere, as though I were like any average girl, who is married and sent off to her husband as soon as, or even before, she finishes her education. But I'm not your average girl! I'm ready and waiting for the chance to establish that there is indeed a need for me to stay right here, in this house. Just as you need me, I need you. It's only on account of mutual need that any relationship based on emotion can endure. Without it, the relationship becomes meaningless. There is no zest in living. Better to do as Akila did. Gulp something down that will put an end to life rather than lead such a humdrum existence.

When the ancient sages perceived that the earth had no further use for them, they would turn their faces northward and prepare to leave earthly life behind. Paati used to say that the soul of such a person would issue forth as a lustrous flame, breaking open the top of the skull. It wasn't difficult to imagine such a scene. I had seen it in many mythological films. Of course, none of these stories changed Paati herself in the least. A couple of minutes before she died, she had gripped Appa's hand and wailed, "Let me have life-giving medicine, da!" What I saw in Appa's eyes was much the same plea for life:

"I suffered terribly without you nearby, Mano!"

Quite suddenly, he had turned into a child. Overcome by a rush of maternal feeling, I caressed his head.

"I'm here now. Stop worrying, you'll be all right."

Yearning intensely for it to really happen that way became fatiguing. Appa was worn out. His eyes drew shut once again. I kept patting his shoulder to soothe him. Unaccustomed though I was to praying, I recited all the names of God that came to my mind. Whole lists of them.

Kamalini stuck her head in. Suddenly, conscious of where I was, I got up and followed her to the verandah outside. "How is he?" she asked.

With great difficulty I held myself in. To stop her seeing that my throat was choked up and my eyes about to brim over, I turned my face away and said, "Not good." She gripped me by the shoulder and gave me a hug. "Be brave. He'll be all right. It's good luck that a hospital was found quickly. What if the heart attack had happened when he was on his way back?" Her words reassured me a little. If that had happened, I would not have had the chance to hear the words he had just spoken to me.

"If anything had happened to him, I would not have been able to bear it, Kamalini."

"I know," she replied briefly. Only a little while ago she had told me that everything I said sounded absurd. What she was saying now was, "I know you love your father so much that you would give up everything for him." It wouldn't have surprised me if she had said I was a psychiatric case. I often felt that about myself! I'd more or less been waiting for a "Certificate of Approval" ever since I had been born, turning myself upside down to get recognition which was not being easily bestowed on me, and I'd more or less been making such acceptance my life's only goal – such an obsession could only be a mental aberration of some kind.

We took a room in a hotel next to the nursing home. Maanikkam said he would sleep in the car and look in on Appa at intervals. At night I tossed about sleeplessly in the midst of the dread about when news would reach me, and what form it would take. It gnawed at me that my decision, and my silent stubbornness may have caused Appa's heart attack. It seemed I had thrown him into a moral dilemma. Perhaps he had felt guilty at his question: "An outsider, to be brought in and installed in the house? How can that be?" The possibility just baffled him.

By daybreak I had resolved to wipe out Shiva's name from my mental dictionary. But Kamalini spoke to me before she set off for Coimbatore. She must have advised me at least a thousand times: "Think about that Hyderabad chap and make a decision!"

"I've forgotten him!" I said, with a smile.

"You are afraid even to think about him!" she retorted, without smiling. But I was in no state of mind to listen to her criticism and analysis.

Appa's condition changed for the better very quickly. The doctor was quite amazed. But whenever he woke up, his eyes would search for me. I put the clinic completely out of my mind and stayed by his side. Maanikkam went back and brought me some clean clothes.

"That Hyderabad person telephoned, Raasamma says. Who is it, Akka?" he enquired.

"Somebody I know," I said.

"All these days he didn't phone, now he is phoning so often?" he persisted.

"Did Raasamma say that?" I asked, dully. "Look here, I have no time to talk about all this. Tell Meenatchi to manage things for some time. No need to take on new cases, or urgent cases at this time."

"All right,' nga, 'ka. If that Ayya rings up again, what shall I say he should be told?"

"Let her tell the truth!" I said with annoyance.

"All these days he didn't phone, now he is phoning so often!" he repeated. I felt like laughing. Raasamma had never fallen in love. Love in the movies was all she knew, all costumed and made-up, the kind of love which runs around some unnatural looking tree, the kind of love that fills duets. She would not understand the ardent passion of a man who was determined to thrust aside all his self-respect, bundling it up and putting it away, just so he could come and live with his wife in her family home. Or maybe they poked around with their questions because they guessed something was going on. I felt embarrassed at the thought of how they would react if they knew that whatever was supposed to be going on had come to an end just as soon as it had begun! Rassamma would certainly feel saddened. "That is what is meant by God's boon, akka – we are destined for only that much!" she would say, finally expounding Vedanta. In my last days, she would be my companion and my support. Amma had died making adhirasams for Appa. It could just be that death would come looking for me while Raasamma and I sat together, two old ladies, watching lovers on TV. But we would never enjoy a renowned place in local history, the way my Amma did.

When it became clear that I wouldn't be returning at once, Sub-inspector Perumaal turned up in Salem to meet me. When so many murder cases remained uninvestigated, it seemed to me that his exertions in the matter of Akila's death were excessive. "What, Perumaal, they're poor people why don't you leave them alone?" I demanded, with some asperity.

"That's not it, Amma. The case has been registered. Afterwards there shouldn't be any doubt, isn't it? The prescriptions you gave are not with them. We told them the body had to be sent for a post-mortem and came away. By the time our fellows went there they had burnt the body."

"They can't read and write, they're poor people. Leave them alone, Perumaal. You have the authority, but please don't display it to them."

Perumaal stood there, hesitantly. "If you give me a letter, I will close the case."

"What sort of letter?"

"That it was a case of natural death due to haemorrhage."

Quietly I wrote down what he wanted on the piece of paper he held out to me, and handed it back to him. As I wrote, my hand shook. "This is my act of repentance," I reflected. I was afraid that I would find myself writing. "I am the one responsible for Akila's death."

They shifted Appa from the I.C.U to the special ward. Although he was still weak, he was encouraged enough by my presence at his side to start saying, "Let's go home. Don't you have to take care of the clinic?"

"Nothing is going to happen if the clinic shuts down for ten days," I answered. "There are other doctors in our town to take care of the sick. But to take care of you, there's only I."

Appa didn't open his mouth. He didn't say, "It's unnecessary trouble for you," and so on. He must have known that such words would hurt me. Or, he might have realized that they'd be meaningless since there wasn't really anyone else who could have taken care of him. We both avoided referring to the argument we had had the previous week, or my silence thereafter. As far as I was concerned, that was a closed chapter. Appa was still in a fragile state of health. I was alert to even the slightest of verbal exchanges which might subject him to emotion. Most of the time after he came home, Appa slept.

He was sleeping now. Sitting in a chair near his hospital bed, reading a magazine my eyes began to close because I had not slept properly the previous night. I put the magazine away and shut my eyes. Effortlessly the body slipped away. Sliding downstream like sand in a river, it crept into a strange cave. The walls of the cave were all scan screens. How many foetuses there were! Manifesting themselves as though magnified to the size of the whole cosmos, they whirled around, their faces hanging down and their buttocks showing. Like upraised tridents, the female genitalia came at me. Their leader Akila approaches. "Your honour, she is a murderess," she says, pointing at me. "Murderess! Murderess!" The tridents cackle. "Order! Order!" shouts the divine judge, tok-tokking his desk. Tok-tok. Tok-tok.

I woke up with a start. It took me a little time to realize where I was. I was hearing a real tok-tok sound. Turning around, I was astounded to see Shiva standing at the door. Fortunately Appa had not woken up. Hurriedly I ran to the door, my heart thumping. I couldn't understand if I felt happy or disturbed at seeing him.

"What, Shiva! All of a sudden?"

He smiled gently. "How is Appa doing?" he asked. The intimacy in his voice made me very uncomfortable. What would he think if I told him, "Even if you condescend to come to me, I am not in a situation to accept you!"

"He is a little better now," I said in a low voice. "He has to stay in hospital for another week. Who told you I was here?"

"I went to your house. Your driver said, `I'm going there now, come with me `nga!' and brough me here."

"Oh!"

"You don't seem very happy to see me!"

Instantly I took a hold on myself. "No, it's just a shock because it's so unexpected. I wasn't expecting you to come down here."

He gave me a tender look. "When I found out you had not

answered my letter because of this sudden crisis, I wanted to see you. Give you some support. Isn't that natural?"

Lacking the courage to look him in the eye, I looked at a distant point and told him, "Thank you, Shiva."

He touched my shoulder. God! I winced. What answer was I going to give him?

"Don't worry," he said comfortingly. 'If good medical care is not available here, we'll take him to Madras. I'll make arrangements."

My father is not willing to believe in you. My calculations were all wrong. Please go away.

Though I wanted to come out with these words quickly, they kept turning and twisting in my throat. Again I said, "Thank you. They are taking good care of him here. He is better now."

"Good! Then why are you looking so sad? Cheer up! Can I see your father?"

I gave a start. "No, no!" I said hurriedly. "He's sleeping."

"Can I see him or not?"

'Yes but...but actually he's asleep."

He walked quietly to the door, looked in, and then turning around flashed me a look.

"He's awake!" he smiled.

A bit disconcerted, I followed him in. Appa looked confused at first. Then he asked me, "Who...?" Before I could introduce him, Shiva came forward.

"I am Shiva. How are you?"

"Who? Oh...!" said Appa, surprised. He looked first at me, then at Shiva. The thought that he might imagine it was I who had summoned Shiva, made me cringe. "He telephoned the house. Raasamma told him what had happened, and he decided to come and see you. I didn't know he was coming," I said, defensively.

Appa nodded weakly, and gestured to Shiva to sit down. Shiva went through Appa's case sheet, looked at the monitor, which was leaping up and down, and remarked, "The treatment they're giving seems to be fine. I was thinking that if necessary we could take you to Madras. That's why I came."

His casual way of talking amazed me. It was quite evident that he had taken it for granted that Appa had accepted him as a son-in-law. With a light pat on Appa's back, he said, "You'll be all right, don't be anxious."

Pa didn't answer but looked keenly at him. The ward ayah peered in. "There's a call for you. `ma." As I hung back, thinking how awkward the interruption was, Shiva said, "You go, I'll be here."

It scared me that Appa might tell him everything. And then he'd get agitated. The situation was a bit out of my control. I ran to take the call. It was a friend of Appa's from out of town who wanted to know how he was. On and on he went, talking in circles. It wasn't easy to extricate myself and hurry back to Appa's room. When I entered, it looked as though they had stopped conversing. They seemed to be sunk in silence. Appa's eyelids were about to close as he descended once more into sleep. Shiva glanced at me, with a little smile. "I'll come and see you in the morning," he said softly. "I have to go and meet someone now."

I did not feel strong enough to go out into the verandah with him. So I stayed where I was and merely nodded . When he had left, I sat there, gazing at Appa, trying to figure out how to manage the situation. What would I say to him if he woke up and demanded: "Did you get him to come here to try and change my mind? Are you trying to take advantage of my weak condition?"

That is why I started, when he said: "We will have the wedding in the month of Chittirai."

Twelve

Maanikkam was driving very carefully. He drives with such skill that travelling in Appa's Contessa was a real pleasure. The car hardly seemed to be moving at all. To make Appa comfortable, I had settled him in the back between bolsters. And had seated myself in front. I kept glancing at him from time to time. I felt a huge sense of relief, but somehow he seemed so fragile. Absorbed in the sights outside, he was gazing out of the window.

"Go to sleep, `pa. I'll wake you up when we're close to town, otherwise you'll get tired." I said.

"I don't want to, amma," he replied, without turning his eyes away. "Can't sleep. I've slept more than enough in the nursing home, haven't I?"

"Ayya, it is only because you have slept and rested that you have at least survived to get up and return home, `nga!" Maanikkam said. His voice sounded unsteady. "That day, I was so afraid! Then, akka arived. As if she had come on wings. If she had not come so fast . . ."

"No need to talk about all that now, Maanikkam," I whispered, with a warning gesture. But Maanikkam was not paying attention. He was engrossed in his own words.

"It had become dark! But akka did not even think about that! She drove down all by herself, ayya!"

"Shh! Maanikkam!" I touched him on the arm to shut him up. I found such praise intensely irritating. It was as though I were being told, "The world doesn't expect such deeds from people like you!" But Maanikkam knew his place. He shut up. Embarrassed, I glanced back at Appa. He was still gazing outside, his lips lifted in a slight smile.

"It was only after I saw her that my life came back, Maanikkam!" he said gently.

I had never heard Appa speak with such emotion. He never came out with his thoughts unless he felt it really necessary to make his opinions known. Again and again the awareness came to me like a rude jolt that he had been really debilitated by the illness that had kept him tied down for ten days in the hospital. I'd felt like this on the day he'd said, from out of the haze of sleep: "We will have the wedding in the month of Chittirai," as though he were saying, "I'll have two biscuits with afternoon coffee." A doubt stuck to me, then: was he really in his senses when he said that? As I slowly took in the words I didn't feel any happiness. Instead I was miserable that he was being pushed into saying this. I did not believe that Shiva could have gained his trust in just five minutes of conversation. It seemed to me that it could only be because he had lost all faith in himself that he had consented to the whole idea.

"We can think about it later, Appa," I said, awakwaardly. "There's no hurry."

Appa smiled weakly. "He looks like a bright fellow all right. And he is somebody you consider acceptable. In the state I am in now, can I afford to be too proud?" Suddenly Appa started crying. I was utterly unnerved, I had never seen him cry before.

Raasamma used to say he wept like a child when my mother died. Maybe she exaggerated. When I got the news and came back from America, I could see from his size that Appa was devastated. He'd lost so much weight. But when he saw me he did not shed a single tear. I put my face in his lap and wept while he stroked my back. "She was a blessed woman, amma. Such a death is not given even to great saints," he told me.

"But why should she die? At just fifty-five?"

Appa was silent for a long time. As he pondered, his hand continued to caress my back.

"There is no answer at all for such a question, amma," he said slowly. "There's no sense in it, either. Even children die. Look at Raasamma's husband – whoosh! Just like a lamp being blown out, he went and died at the age of thirty-two. I can see only one meaning from all this: death will come at any time! One must be ready for it."

I remember sitting up with a jerk.

"You are not reassuring me. You are terrifying me!"

Appa laughed gently. "If you reflect a bit, you will understand that what I have said are reassuring words."

To what extent had he been able to reassure himself? I didn't quite know. Certainly his conversation, and his general good cheer were greatly reduced. He had no taste left for food.

But even before this setback in his health, I'd had the feeling that he had lost interest in everything. That is, until he had said, so firmly and unmistakably: *This is my house*.

Between wisdom and renunciation there is considerable difference. A man with rich holdings in several cotton mills may talk philosophy, but he cannot become an anchorite. Nor is there any need for him to do so. But Appa seemed to think the need had now arisen. Like Dasaratha deciding that it was time to perform Rama's coronation, when he noticed a grey hair near his ear. In Appa's eyes, however, there now flickered shadows cast by the fear of dying. He was like one defeated and disarmed, one who tormentedly cries, "I cannot fight any more!" His chest heaved weakly.

I held him close and wiped the tears from his eyes.

"There is nothing wrong with you. Why should you feel so weak? You will be all right. I am here, aren't I?"

Appa's sobs slowly subsided. I didn't have to look very far to discover the reason for his change of heart. It was fear, fear because he was now conscious of his need to have me by his side. If I were to stay with him, then there was no way but to allow a stranger in the house. An 'outsider'. Thoughtfully I gazed at him as he once again sank wearily into sleep. With a pang, I thought, if I take advantage of this frailty of his, it will be demeaning for him.

The next day Shiva showed up, as he'd said he would. He made known his love for me with his eyes. He often ventured to touch me as he talked. I couldn't respond the same way. If Appa's heart attack had been a climax, his statement "We will have the wedding in Chittirai" made it seem strangely like an anti-climax.

"Did your father ask you anything about my letter?" he asked.

"He said he wouldn't be able to say anything until he met you," I lied. Playfully twirling a curl close to my ear around his finger, he smiled.

"What does he say now?"

"He says we can have the wedding in Chittirai!"

'Ah ha haa!" He laughed a hero's laugh. Encircling my waist, he leaned close to my ear, as if about to kiss me, and whispered, "In just five minutes I was able to straighten your father out. For five years I couldn't do that with you!" Flustered by his hot breath and his touch, I released myself, saying, "This is a hospital; Shiva!"

"Then come outside!"

"I can't leave Appa and come. When he opens his eyes he will look around for me."

For moment he gazed intensely at me. Then smiling slightly, he patted me on the back, "Áll right, as you wish. Chittirai is not far ahead. I'll be coming here often. I've got a plan to set up practice in Salem. I have to start doing certain things in order to wind up in Hyderbad and restart here. Isn't Salem just an hour-long drive from your village?"

"Can't you do all that after the wedding?" I smiled uncertainly. "Chittirai means it will be very soon. Let Appa get better. We'll have the wedding after that. We've waited all this time. What's another two or three months?"

"Okay. No problem," he said in English, easily. "But I'm going to start my work here. Any objection?"

"No, Shiva," I said, head bowed. Then I looked up, and asked, carefully threading one word with another. "You've thought carefully about it before coming to this decision, haven't you, Shiva?"

"Absolutely," he said, again in English. "Why, do you have any doubts?"

Again I bowed my head. "If one day you feel it was wrong to have left Hyderabad, I will die of guilt." Again he caught hold of me by the waist and drew me close to him.

"So, I'll grant you a boon of immortality! Don't talk such silly nonsense! I have the capacity. Why should I be afraid of anything?"

He must have come out with a hundred words of encouragement before he finally took himself off. Although he was so cheerful and so exuberant, I felt uncertain. Did I deserve any of this? If I were to tell Kamalini of my conflicting feelings, she'd probably laugh. "Did you consider all this when you laid down that condition of yours?" she would mock. True, I hadn't done so. Until the moment that Shiva gave in to the condition that I had laid down, I'd been at peace.

"Maanikkam, switch off the AC and roll down the window, please," said Appa.

"Why, 'pa, are you feeling cold?" I asked anxiously.

"No, 'ma," he replied, his eyes fixed outside. "I want to breathe in the smell of our land."

That was when I noticed that we had reached the outskirts of our town. Adjoining the highway were Appa's lands, far-flung and extensive. Half had come to him as ancestral property, the rest he had earned himself. How he managed his land and his cotton factories had never interested me until now. He had trustworthy agents to administer his properties. "Anybody who actually has intentions to swindle Ayya wouldn't be able to do it, `nga!" they often declared. "Not even the smallest mistake escapes his eyes."

And this was the man who had now become so weak that he could say, "In the state I am now in, can I afford to be too proud?" If he had had a son instead of me, he would have felt quite differently, I thought. In place of mere paid supervisors, he would have had his own son. He could have shared confidential business information with him. There would have been no opportunity to feel mocking self-pity about his "fine condition". What he would have felt instead would have been: "I have a strong son, like Bhima himself! What more can I ask!" He'd have relaxed, and just closed his eyes.

Now, when death's knife was poised at his throat, all his old fears were back to haunt him.

It was only when I saw her that my life came back to me.

I had been waiting to hear this for so long. For him to accept me as a part of himself. And yet my mind did not strap on its wings and take flight! I am conscious that this, too, arises from his sense of being limited.

"Have you ever read Superman comics?" demanded Appa, suddenly.

"Oh?" I replied, astonished. "Yes, I've read them."

"When we were youngsters, my friends and I would go all the way to Salem, just to see the Superman films in English. Superman is a super hero. It was our dream to be like him. We believed that the actor who was playing Superman was Superman himself. You know, on the day that he killed himself, it was as though God himself had died."

Why was Appa remembering this now? It mystified me. He did not offer any explanation, he just sat there smiling to himself. Maanikkam gave me a worried glance. When we had almost reached home, Appa said: "Why I am saying this is because we all think of ourselves as Superman. But that's only a role—just like in the cinema." By the time I pulled myself together to make a response, we were at the house.

I was startled to see a number of people in the compound, sitting around here and there. Each one had turned up to enquire after Appa's health, and to express their regret at his illness. Fearing that their concern and affection would completely finish him off, weak as he was, I jumped down from the car and hurried towards them. "If you crowd around like this, Appa will get exhausted!" I said, addressing them all together. "Please, everyone, come and see him later. Right now he needs rest."

"All right, `nga, 'mma," said one old woman. "We'll just stand at a distance and take a look and go away." Appa was helped out of the car into a chair. Maanikkam and two others carried him into the house. His business managers were waiting inside. "We will talk tomorrow," Appa told them.

Satisfied that they had seen him alive, the gathering gradually dispersed. We settled him comfortably in bed, in his own room. I went downstairs to tell them what to cook for the evening meal and then sat at the dining table. All the strength in my body seemed to have drained out.

"Bring me some coffee, Raasamma," I said. "At night Appa should have only two idlis. And buttermilk, with all the butter taken out."

"All right, `nga,'kka," said Raasamma. She brought steaming hot coffee and put it in front of me saying, "In these past ten days, you have become half your size, akka."

"This body of mine has got used to eating food cooked by

your hand, oh?" I laughed. "What's the matter, why is your face looking different? Have you been crying?"

She wiped her eyes with the end of her sari. "All of us felt very bad when we saw Ayya!"

I finished drinking the coffee in silence. Then I said, "He will have to be careful from now on, Raasamma. No oil, no ghee. No coconut. You must be very particular about his diet. You better not throw in lots of ghee and *paruppu*, thinking he must get back his energy!"

"Ayye!" said Raasamma, making a face. "I will do as you say. What a good thing you studied to become a doctor – that is what we have all been saying."

"But I didn't give medical treatment to Appa."

"So what if you didn't? Didn't you run to his side and take care of him, just like a man?"

Oh, God! Again the same thing. I got up.

"Did anyone come to see me while I was away?"

"That Hyderabad person came. Who is he, akka?"

"Just someone I know.

"He was so casual. He asked for a cup of coffee as though he had every right! I made it and served him. When Maanikkam said he was going to Salem, at once he said he'd go with him."

Her voice was full of enthusiasm – almost too much, I thought.

"Were there any other visitors?"

"Oh, I forgot. That policeman turned up here."

"Perumaal?"

"Yes. Asking hundreds of questions! I told him – you're in such a rush, why don't you go to Salem and see Amma and ask her yourself. Some law or other he was going on about. As though he's a very honourable man himself."

Meddlesome woman, had she gone and blurted out something? I had no interest in unearthing gossip about Perumaal.

Appa was sleeping. I thought of the story of Superman that he had told me. Tomorrow when the work in the nursing home gets over I must talk to his supervisors, I thought. For a woman who has studied medicine and runs a nursing home, management whether it is of a cotton-ginning mill or of a farm, isn't an esoteric science. If Appa imagined that his dream of Superman had died, he had only himself to blame. Nostalgia for tales of ancient times, for legends and epics, was his forte. It made me furious to have to clean them off him —take a wet cloth and wipe the slate clean!

Kamalini once told me there was a poem in the *Puranas*, known as the *Adhbhuta Ramayanam*. There, it was not Rama who killed Ravana. It was Sita who, when Rama fainted, took up his bow and killed Ravana. This must have been written by a woman – or women – who didn't want to make a hero out of a man who sent away his wife on the strength of hearsay. It made me laugh. "Why couldn't this have been the original story?" Kamalini had demanded.

Thirteen

As I stepped out of Appa's airconditioned room into the central area of the mill, the sound drilled into my ears, even before the heat hit me. Workers stood around watching the rapid twirling of the spinning shuttles, their faces registering astonishment when they saw me. Bringing their hands together in greeting, they tried to brush away the cotton fluff clinging to their heads, faces, arms and legs. Supervisor Thanikachalam raised his voice above the noise of the machines to explain everything to me, as though I was visiting a cotton-spinning mill for the first time. Barely listening to his words, I was looking instead at the workers, moving on, and smiling a little. The lesson was elementary and one that I didn't need, but I mustn't be in a hurry to tell him that. A little earlier he and another manager, Sambandham, had presented me with a bare outline of Appa's industrial activities. As though they considered it unnecessary for me to know more than that.

"You don't need to worry about all this, *thangachchi*[2]! Until Ayya is up and about, we will take care of everything, nothing will be neglected," declared Thanikachalam.

"I know you will. But I just want to learn. There is nothing wrong with that, is there?"

"Chhe chhe! What can be wrong with that?" said Sambandham, pushing himself forward. You already have so much work at the clinic, if you get into this also, you won't know where all your time has gone – that's what we mean to say!"

It's always possible to find time," I said, smiling. "As his daughter, it seems to me that I should help my father as much as I can. I don't want him to feel disheartened and say, 'What do you know, amma, about the mill!'"

"Isn't it likely that in a few days he may start coming to the office?" asked Thanikachalam, doubtfully.

"It will take some time. He needs to rest at least for a month," I said carefully avoiding any display of emotion. And even afterwards I feel he should stop coming to the mill. I can come and look after things as his representative." Noticing their exchange of looks, I felt a grating uncertainty in my mind. I had rubbed them up the wrong way. This arrangement did not please them. I knew there was no reason hidden behind their disapproval, they fully deserved Appa's trust. The problem was simply that they saw no need for a woman to stick her nose into a man's realm.

"By all means!" replied Thanikachalam, his perplexity visible on his face. "Please feel free to come and reassure yourself. If Ayya says yes, then it is yes."

They are testing me, I thought, trying to see how far I'll go. Perhaps they think Appa has sent me because he does not trust them. But if I had told Appa I was coming here, he would have said, "What for, amma? The two of them will take care of things." And if I had countered, "It is good for me to know about these matters, Appa," he would have been greatly perturbed.

The mill workers stood up as I approached and greeted me with vanakkams. It was mortifying — as if I were insinuating myself into alien territory. I imagined myself, in their eyes —an unsuitable, unauthorised candidate for Appa's position, attempting to usurp it even before his death.

I climbed into Appa's Contessa. Thanikachalam and Sambandham seemed sunk in thought as they watched Maanikkam starting the car.

"Maanikkam, please wait a bit," I said. Lowering the window,

I looked at them and smiled shyly. "Appa did not send me here. He does not even know that I am here," I told them.

"What does that matter, thangachchi? Please come any time you want," Sambandham said. Yet in both faces there was a perceptible easing of tension.

"To the clinic?" asked Maanikkam.

"Yes," I replied.

A feeling of terrible humiliation came over me. Despite being Appa's daughter, my sudden arrival had been seen as an intrusion and had given rise to feelings of suspicion. "Here, in this environment, your status amounts to no more than this."

Slowly I calmed myself. Coming here without any warning had been a mistake. If these people thought I had come to proclaim my authority as the heiress-apparent to the throne, there was nothing surprising in it. That I could be genuinely interested in finding out how things were run at the mill, that my intention was serious was something they wouldn't understand. They might be of the opinion that for me, these matters were not only unnecessary but also beyond my comprehension. Conscious that I knew nothing of Appa's plans for the future, I felt troubled. What did he think would happen to the mill after him? Sambandham and Thanikachalam were assistants – they were not partners. Although his heart attack had been unexpected, it seemed unlikely that he had not thought about all this.

I shrank from having to ask him about it, face to face

This sensitivity, this timidity was a curse on me, from my very birth. If I'd been a man, would I have hesitated to do every single thing like this? The comparison seemed odious!

"Don't just let the fort slip out of your hands, you have a right to this house." As though it were just yesterday I remembered how Amma had sat before me and spoken each word with deliberate emphasis, as though she were pulling them taut like string. She couldn't have known that those words would have a magnetic,

hypnotic power over me. She couldn't have imagined the sort of stimulus those words had provided me. Uneducated as she was she would not have understood that these words had not been spoken to me alone, as an individual woman.

"When they saw the car in the mill compound, many people rushed up so eagerly, thinking Ayya had come," said Maanikkam.

"Mm..." I said, deep in thought.

"They just besieged me with questions!"

"About what?"

"'Is Chinnamma getting married?' they wanted to know."

It gave me a terrific jolt. I had not breathed a word about this to anybody. Had Appa told his people at the office then?

"What did you tell them?" I said, embarrassed.

"I told them I don't know. But they did not believe me. They are saying that the Hyderabad doctor is going to be the bridegroom. Is that true?"

"Nothing has been decided yet, Maanikkam. Let Appa's health get better first."

"Ayya will be fine. And, should you postpone auspicious events just for that?" advised Maanikkam, sounding a hundred years old. "It will be a very suitable match, akka, very fine!" He said with enthusiasm. "Even at the mill, that is what they were saying."

"How do they know?"

"Why it seems the bridegroom ayya came here yesterday." I was dumbfounded. I couldn't understand why Shiva had turned up here. He hadn't mentioned that he planned to come. I wasn't in yesterday when he'd arrived at the house. I'd gone to Thimmampatti on an urgent case, and it was quite late when I returned. Appa said he had looked in on him before he left.

"He seems to have settled down in Salem?"

"Yes. I even told him not to be in such a hurry. But he told me that he needs time to set up his practice," he said.

"He looks like a lively sort of fellow," remarked Appa. I couldn't make out if he meant this as praise or criticism.

"Those who have grown up in the city are like that."

For a while Appa did not say anything at all. Then, as though he had thought deeply about it, he said, "It will be good if the wedding takes place soon."

"No! There is no hurry," I said firmly. "It will take place only after you are up and feeling normal."

"This is a small town. He'll turn up here every day and hang around waiting to see you. It will not be proper." Suppressing my annoyance, I said, "Is that what you're worried about? I will tell him that until we're married he should not come around to see me!"

Appa smiled slightly, as if he did not believe a word I was saying.

Now, why was he going to the mill and making an exhibition of himself as the future son-in-law? It made me furious. Would he understand if I told him that this excessive 'liveliness' of his would plunge me into a difficult situation, a conflict of loyalties? I doubted it. An explanation seemed to be emerging for the confusion that had cast such shadows in Thanikachalam's eyes, and darkened Sambandham's glance. Even to have travelled in Appa's car had been an impertinence! I felt ashamed.

At the clinic, Meenatchi informed me of two emergency cases. "One is a delivery, the other is an abortion. I don't know which one to attend to first!"

I hastened inside. The woman who was in labour was unable even to bear down, she was so weak. Calculating that it would take at least another hour before she was ready, I went to see the other case. Astonished to find Shanbagam writhing in pain, I demanded, "Shanbagam? What's happened to you? That day I gave you something for it, didn't I? Didn't it come out?"

She shook her head to say no.

"Then why didn't you come again?"

She was unable to reply. In a soft voice, Meenatchi said, "When Ayya's health was bad, you were not here. She went to a local medicine woman and swallowed something or other."

"Ah di! You awful creature!" I cursed in an undertone. There was no doctor in this place, apart from me, to whom she would have had the courage to show her face. Abusing all silly women who get themselves into such awkward situations, I gave her a sedative and got down to the job.

Meenatchi whispered in the middle of it: "Who do you think is the cause of all this, `nga?"

"What does it matter who it is? Some scoundrel," I said, wearily.

"It is a fellow who goes around as though he is a very honourable man," said Meenatchi.

Honourable.

I was startled. Raasamma had used the same word.

"Who? Is it Perumaal?"

"Yes, correct! How did you guess?"

"How did she get herself caught by him?"

"Ask her."

"Look here, when the sedative wears off, she'll try to get up and go home. Let her stay here for two days. She needs rest." It was time now to go in to see the labour case.

I could not talk any more. Since the woman did not have the strength to cooperate, I had finally to use forceps to remove the infant. Wearily I noted how she dropped off to sleep with relief as soon as she found out it was a male child. When I came outside, my eyes fell on Shanbagam's inert form. I thought of Perumaal. He was a married man. I was outraged: how could this woman let herself get trapped by him? When I had asked her the last time she came here, she hadn't answered, I remembered how she had wept. Tomorrow when she is a little stronger I must ask her again, I thought. Sleeping, she looked pitiable. Her work-hardened, firm-fleshed physique now resembled the tattered fibres of a reed.

It seemed like a long time since I had seen Appa, so, I left for the house. On the clinic verandah sat Paavayee, threading a garland of pink oleander blossoms. "It is Full Moon pujai today, Amma, for Mangamma Thayee. You must come," she said, when she saw me.

"Special pujai," Meenatchi put in. "For Periayya's recovery and return home."

"'Special'? What are you going to do?" I asked.

"We will offer pongal. I'll send Muniappan to fetch you," said Paavaayee.

I don't have the faith that these women have. Yet why does this act of worship make me go soft inside? I can't understand it. Whether or not Paavaayee regards this pujai as social service, what it has done is to create a feeling of togetherness among the women here. It is Paavaayee's belief that the normal deliveries and the birth of male babies in this clinic are all traceable to Mangamma's blessing.

Calling out to Raasamma to ask if Appa had eaten and slept, I climbed upstairs. Appa was reclining in his bed with a newspaper in his hand.

"So, Appa? You are reading the paper?" I said.

"I can only manage to read a little bit, then I get tired," he said despondently. "When will I become normal, amma?"

I said, "You will get better gradually, Appa." I felt sad. "You shouldn't be in a hurry. Or let yourself get depressed."

"Of course, it is depressing. I have never stayed in bed like this."

"Can't be helped. The body can't always be the same, can it?"

"Dignity is possible only if one is strong and sturdy until the last breath, amma!"

"Why are you talking like this?" I scolded. "You've plenty of dignity. Rest for a few days and you will soon be just the same as you used to be!"

Appa did not reply. He leaned against the wall and closed his eyes. I went close to him and gripped his shoulders.

"Why, Appa, what has happened today? Why are you talking like this? Are you in pain?"

"No, no nothing like that. But I feel very tired. When I think how many days I'm going to be like this, it is just too much."

"You'll be fine, you'll get energy if you eat properly and take your medicines," I said, stroking his forehead. "You are bored! That's the problem."

Appa opened his eyes and chuckled lightly. "That's true enough."

"I'll ask Maanikkam to stay here, and read to you from the paper, from books. I don't need him," I said.

"Did you go to the mill today?" Appa asked. "Any reason?"

"No, nothing particular. I thought if I'm familiar with it, I can be of some use to you when the need arises."

Appa did not say anything.

"It's good to learn, is it not?"

"Yes. It's good," he said slowly. "I never thought about all this. Thanikachalam and Sambandham shouldn't think you are interfering."

"It is for you to remove their doubts."

"Hold on for a few days. If you are seen to be in a hurry, there will only be confusion."

My head bowed. I said sadly, "Why should I be in a hurry?" I was embarrassed by the thought that they must have told him about Shiva's visit to the mill. Appa looked disturbed. Looking out of the window, I saw that Muniappan had come to fetch me.

I turned to Appa. "It's full moon tonight. They are doing a pujai. I'll be back soon." Then, with a vehemence new to me I said, "I remember Paati. When I said I wanted to study, she said, 'just because you study, you can't change into a man!' Today I understand what she meant. She was not talking about physical form. She was talking about ideas."

As I came down the stairs and walked along with Muniappan, I heard the women ululating.

I had a feeling that tonight Mangamma Thayee would not be the only one to put in an appearance. My mother, too, would be there.

Fourteen

In the light of the full moon they all looked spectral, not human. Oblivious that I had come and was standing right there, they were staring intently at "Mangamma", who was wreathed in pink oleander, streaked yellow with *manjal* paste, with bright-red kumkumam [3] slapped on. There was a sheen on Paavaayee's cheeks, shrunken and shrivelled up as she was. With arms outspread and sobbing effortlessly, she cried out: "Save us, Thayee!" Inexplicably my hair stood on end, as I stared at them standing there with tears coursing down their faces. I seemed to have caught the contagion of their hysteria.

O Lady, you endowed us with life, as alms.
Like milk for a burning stomach, you are a balm.

Thrilling with the lyric impulse, Paavaayee finished with a mighty wail:

"We have no refuge but you, Mother!" The others moaned: "With folded hands we hail you, Mother!" before they, at, last dropped down and worshipped the stone. The pongal they had prepared, spending what little cash was in their hands, the fruit, the coconuts, the incense and the smoke —all of it seemed as though sanctified by their inner purity. If Descartes said, "I think, therefore I am," I told myself, these people believe, therefore Mangamma exists.

Raasamma has been devoutly observing this ritual, year after year on Amma's death anniversary. "Amma is coming tomorrow," she would remind me the day before. This Mangamma pujai began quite recently, after I had had the nursing home built and set up practice. It seems Paavaayee had a dream in which Mangamma appeared. There was no history of Mangamma here before that. Raasamma offered an explanation: "It could have been Amma, who appeared in the dream." It made me want to laugh. Why should *my* mother appear in Paavaayee's dream? So far she has never appeared in any dream of mine!

But today, in this spooky company, I had a hallucination — I said Amma. There she stood. "I have failed, Amma! " I confessed to the apparition. "If I raise myself up by a handsbreadth, I slide back by a whole armlength! Why did you tie me down like this? What did you want me to achieve? You knew this is a war – I saw shadows, and yet you urged me on, as though you were ignorant, as if you were a simpleton!"

"It's up to you to show how smart you are, and win this war," Amma said, leaving me to deal with the burden of these women who were at this very moment dissolving eerily in the moonlight, and making me feel so very, very tired.

Gana-gana-gana...someone was clanging a bell. I came out of my trance. Like some priest of ripe experience, Paavaayee was flourishing a tray with a bit of burning camphor above and below and on either side of the bedaubed stone, waving it this way and that, with her face shining in the light of the flame. She is conducting this pujai solely because of the feeling of importance it gives her. Mangamma, who sprang forth from Paavaayee's imagination, has become everybody's burden-bearing stone, like one of those erected by the wayside by old time kings for footsore travellers to set down their bundles. And odd as it is, she has obtained my patronage as well.

From among the cluster of women standing there, one woman suddenly slithered down. "Ayyo! Ayyo!" the women panicked, as I sprang forward. As two women held up the fainting Shanbagam, I took her pulse. Her body felt hot as fire.

"Lift her up and take her inside. Who allowed her to come here?" I scolded, directing my wrath at everybody in general.

"I didn't even notice her coming and standing here, akka!" Meenatchi said. Two others lent a hand as she hurried to get Shanbagam into the clinic.

A great commotion was perceptible among the women, as they began to hiss and buzz among themselves. Their whispers reached my ears.

"Pujai is over, no? Get back to your jobs, every one of you!" I bawled at them once again.

Paavaayee's face had fallen. Paying no attention, I went into the clinic.

Shanbagam's condition worried me. She had a fever of a hundred and five degrees. Having arrived with a septic abortion, she was in such a state that the treatment I was administering did not have a satisfactory effect. Her condition must have been even worse than I had thought.

"Did you give her the medicines like I told you, Meenatchi?" I queried.

"Yes, 'nga,'ka." Meenatchi rubbed Shanbagam's hands to warm them. "With high fever she came and was standing outside with the dew falling, yet none of us even noticed!" Ignoring her lament, I began emergency procedures. The fever had to be brought down. At once. A little later Shanbagam came out of her faint and opened her eyes. She gazed around, dazed, and tried to break free of Meenatchi's grasp and get up. I held her tight and made her lie down.

"It is nothing, Shanbagam. Don't be afraid. You will be all right. Just lie down quietly. If you rest you will be all right."

She gave me a fixed stare. "I have to go. They are calling me."

"Nobody is calling you. Lie down," Meenatchi told her. Shanbagam looked at me pleadingly . "They are calling. Periamma is calling."

Meenatchi glanced at me. "Periamma has been dead for a long time, Shanbagam," she said mildly.

"It's her. She's standing there!" Even if Shanbagam was only blabbering because of the fever, her talking about Amma today of all days was absurdly unsettling. "Look here, whoever comes, you must not get up and go off! You have a fever." I told her sternly.

For a little while Shanbagam lay there panting and gasping. When the fever slowly subsided, she stared at me like one who has just become conscious. She looked as though tears were imminent. I patted her shoulder soothingly.

"You will be all right. Don't worry."

Desperately she caught my hands. "No, Akka! No need for me to get all right. I must die!"

"Chhee chhee! Don't! Pain gives you one little prick, and just for that you want to die?" I said, remembering Akhila. Shanbagam shook her head from side to side and wept, tears streaming from her eyes.

"It's better for me to die."

"If you talk like this one more time I will get angry!" I told her. "From now on you have to see to it that nothing wrong happens. That's in your hands alone."

Her grip on my hands grew tighter. She looked so anguished that it startled me.

"I can't, akka. I can't. I have to tell you, akka, before I close my eyes."

"Please go out," I told Meenatchi. When she had left, I said, "You will be all right, Shanbagam. Tell me — what is your problem?"

"I cannot stop doing wrong, akka. That man is fooling me. He tempts me saying he will get me contracts..."

"Who is it?"

"Policeman. Perumaal."

"Why do you go? Why do you trust him?"

Loosening her grip on me, she began to strike herself on the head, with great slamming blows. With great difficulty I restrained her hands. Convulsed and shaking with sobs, she cried, "This body of mine is shameless, akka. It wants to…what can I do?"

I sat there, shocked. I remembered what I had asked her the last time: "Why can't you just – leave it all to…to God, or whoever — and just get married, Shanbagam?" How she had broken into tears. To tell her to get a grip on herself seemed idiotic at such a time. Her guilt was enough to kill her, it seemed to me. Gently I stroked her fiery-hot forehead. "We will talk about all this in the morning. Now you need rest. When you get a little strength we will see how to solve this problem." Keeping the conversation going awhile, I gave her a sedative. Gradually her agitation subsided.

When her eyes closed and she began to fall asleep I came out. The women were still standing around talking in low voices. Infuriated, I shouted, "Standing around and gossipping! Don't you have any other work? Get out!" The very sight of me sent them scattering.

"Will you have some pongal, amma?" Paavaayee held out a piece of banana leaf. I took a little pongal from it and popped it into my mouth, accepted the kumkumam and the flowers she offered me, and told her, "You go, too, Paavaayee…. When a woman has got caught in a difficult situation, you don't give any sympathy, any of you. All you'll do is gossip."

"It is not gossip, Amma," said Paavaayee, with dignity. "From a burning stomach we are talking A man's work she was doing — how proud we felt! But now, we feel like telling her: 'Oh you sinful creature, you have gone and spoilt your good name, di!'"

I did not say anything. After instructing Kala, the nurse on night duty, to be extra vigilant, I left. The full implications of Paavaayee's words struck me with renewed ferocity. I kept remembering Perumaal's expression of overweening self-confidence, and the ease with which he talked about The Law.

When I got home, a shock awaited me. Shiva was sitting in the middle of the hall, watching TV. Involuntarily I looked at the clock. Nine-thirty. Why had he turned up at this hour?

" Hi!" he said in the American manner, grinning enticingly, and going on to demand "Why so late?" as though his arrival were expected. Raasamma looked a little confused and embarrassed. Smiling at me, she enquired, "The pujai took such a long time, amma?"

"A complicated case turned up, all of a sudden," I said, my eyes on Shiva. "When did you come?" I asked him.

"An hour ago."

"Did you give him anything, Raasamma? Tiffin, coffee?" I enquired.

"He wanted to wait till you came, akka, he told me," Raasamma said, and began to lay the plates on the table. "Please come, everything is ready."

"Has Appa had his food? Did you give him medicine?"

"I have, akka. He is sleeping."

"I'll just be back, Shiva," I said, and quickly went upstairs to Appa's room. Appa's anxiety of that morning came back to me. "He'll turn up every day and hang around waiting to see you." I felt like giggling. Having turned up at such an hour, when would he leave? Appa was asleep. There were traces of his having taken the medicines. I made a noiseless exit.

Going up to the table I looked at everything laid out and said to Raasamma, "I'll manage. You go and watch TV." She took the hint and moved off. Maanikkam must definitely have informed her that Shiva was the prospective son-in-law of the house.

"I'm really hungry!" said Shiva. Without the least bashfulness or hesitation he helped himself and proceeded to eat. As for me,

I didn't know where my appetite had gone, thanks to the experiences I had had all day.

"You never told me you were coming!" I said, again.

Abruptly he looked up. "Why, are you saying I should not come without telling you?" The anger in his voice was new to me.

"Chhe Chhe! That wasn't what I meant! If I had known you were coming I would have adjusted my work accordingly. Of course, if an emergency case turns up, that is another matter."

With a wave of his hands, "No adjustment necessary," he said, charmingly. "The fellow who's going to adjust is me!"

Quickly shoving aside the thought that he would weaken me with this one weapon alone, I smilingly remarked, "Then there is no problem! I needn't be overcome by a feeling of guilt!"

"Correct!" he replied in English, and continued to eat heartily.

"Have you found a place in Salem to start the clinic?"

"I'm still looking around," he said, nodding vigorously. "It'll be found."

"In which place?"

"There are four or five possible locations. I have to see which suits me best."

"I heard you went to Appa's mill?" I ventured, as though off-hand. He looked up at me and gave an easy laugh. "Oh, yes. I was going that way and thought, let me go in and take a look. D'you know, I have never seen a spinning mill before?"

Without answering, I continued to eat, a half-smile on my face.

"You know those secretaries of your father's – that mill doesn't need security guards at all, they will do fine for that job. How they poked and prodded me to find out who I was!"

"They've been there for many years," I explained with a smile.

"I can see that."

I did not know what he meant by saying that. Getting up

from the table, we went back to the hall. "You go and eat," I told Raasamma, sending her away.

"Let's go upstairs and talk," Shiva whispered. "We can't get cosy in front of this cook-woman of yours, can we?"

"What a time you've chosen to get cosy!" I laughed uncomfortably.

"Can there be a better time than this? The moon is shining, and the whole town's asleep."

"Where do you plan to spend the night?" I asked guardedly.

"Here! Where else?" he retorted, as though I had asked a really silly question.

"I've no objection to your staying here. There's a guest-room downstairs," I said timidly.

"Okay, thank you," he said in English, without removing his gaze from the TV screen. "So then you're saying there's no need to go upstairs and talk?"

"No need," I said firmly. "I'm very sleepy. There's a serious case today. I might get a call in the middle of the night. Only if I sleep a little now will I be able to work tomorrow."

"Okay," he said, shrugging his shoulders. "I can adjust."

Still with a smile on my face, I went into the guest-room to see if the sheets were all right, and if there was a towel and soap in the bathroom. I felt nervous that he might indulge in loverlike antics in front of Raasamma. And I was genuinely tired and sleepy.

"Let's talk tomorrow, Shiva. I'll have some drinking water brought to you. Good night." I said, and went to Raasamma to tell her about his staying the night. She listened quietly and said, "All right, 'ngakka."

Upstairs, I took Appa's cordless phone to my room and kept it close to my bed, changed and lay down. For a couple of minutes there was a gnawing thought that Shiva might be offended at my abruptly ending the conversation and coming away like this. But I was so excessively fatigued that sleep quickly claimed me.

In the middle of the night, when I was deep in sleep the telephone rang, shaking me awake. Switching on the table-lamp, I said, "Hello?" It was Kala from the clinic, and her voice sounded agitated. "Come immediately, akka. That Shanbagam is bleeding badly. Body is jerking, she is having fits," she said.

"I'm coming," I replied, took my flashlight and set off. It was two o'clock when I reached the clinic. Shanbagam was in a terrible condition. The bed and the sari she wore were soaked in blood. Her pulse had all but stopped, her chest heaved up and down, and her eyes were rolling upwards. She was unrecognizable. Panic gripped me in the pit of my stomach. Until now, no case of mine had ever let me down like this. None of the emergency procedures was of any help.

"No, Shanbagam, you mustn't die, you mustn't!" Even as I kept muttering these words, almost in a chant, her breathing ceased. The sight of that bed drenched in blood turned my stomach.

"Just write that it was a natural death, due to bleeding."

That was what Perumaal had said. And dazedly I repeated the same words to Kala. She wrote them down in the register.

Utterly worn out, I reached home. What Paavaayee had said, "From a burning stomach we are talking" was true. My eyes seemed crammed with tears, pushing and straining to escape. I went soundlessly up the stairs in the dark. As I leaned back in bed, "Where did you go at this hour of the night?"came Shiva's voice, in a sibilant whisper.

It gave me an awful shock. Like being seized unceremoniously and flung down from a great height.

I switched on the table lamp.

Fifteen

With his arms crossed under his head, Shiva lay lounging on my bed. The sight of him, bare-chested, a lungi wrapped around his waist, made me flinch. A never-before-felt fury blazed up in me at the realization that he had obviously come with the intention of staying. Aware that my fingers were trembling, I hid them by gripping the table hard and leaning back against it.

"It's just me. Put off the light," he said, as though exercising what was his right. Then, in a soft voice, "You're a doctor – yet you're so scared!"

I stayed where I was. Suppressing my fury I said, "Shiva. Please go away."

"Chhee chhee, don't act like a villager, put off the light. By the time that cook-girl wakes up, I'll be back in my room, don't worry."

"I am not worried about that."

"Then what is it?" he teased, lightly. "In two months, we are going to be husband and wife. You're an educated woman. Yet just like any village girl you stand there looking so terrified!"

I was so fatigued in mind and body that I was in no condition to enter into an argument with him. Shanbagam's blood was not yet dry on my hands, it seemed to me.

"Shiva, please, I don't want to get into a discussion. Please go to your room. I am very tired."

Swiftly he rose and came close to me. He placed his hands on the table on either side of me as I stood leaning against it so that I couldn't move. "I'll remove that tiredness, kannu," he whispered near my ear, and deftly reached behind me to switch off the table-lamp. I became aware that I couldn't break free, caught as I was in his iron grip.

"No, Shiva, no, please," I said, trying to turn my face away. But his hand was upon my chin, forcing it to turn back. Hot with passion, his lips pressed down upon my lips, I seemed to be burning and shrivelling up in that fire. His touch, and his caress and whispered "kannu" made me dizzy. Deep down in my belly I could feel myself tremble.

"Shiva, you should know me better. I'm in no mental condition for this today, please go." My voice threatened to betray how vulnerable my body had become.

"I understand that. That's why you need me tonight. You just go to sleep. Don't talk. Come." As though he were leading a child, he walked me to the bed and made me lie down. Exhausted, I closed my eyes — in the stupid belief that he would go away…

"You go to sleep, kannu. Don't worry about me. As soon as you're asleep, I'll go away," he said, stroking me gently. Sleep would not come. As his warm fingers roamed wider and wider over my skin, sensations that had lain dormant thrilled awake, looming over me like devils, crowning themselves with those hissing whispers of his — `Kannu! Kannu!" In spite of myself, they were breaking out, like Shiva's elemental hordes let loose.

I could see this…I could actually see this happening.

"This body is shameless, akka. It wants to…"

A pang went through me. "Shanbagam, don't cry!" I wanted to say. There's no connection between honour and decency and…this…I wanted to tell her. Even now, in certain African countries women's private parts are mutilated to suppress their desire for sex.

"How cruel," I murmured.

"Very cruel," replied Shiva. "How many years you've been testing my patience! For your sake I have accepted all your conditions and come here. *That* you should never forget,"

I sprang awake, as though branded with a hot iron, shook off his arm and jumped down. Slapping on the switch near the door, I lit up the room. Thoroughly unnerved, he stared at me.

"Ei, what's wrong with you, suddenly?" he said, weakly. Setting right my dishevelled hair and disordered clothes I told him sternly, but in a low voice, "Go away, Shiva. I cannot allow you in here. You cannot do anything against my consent, sorry. If you don't leave the room I shall go and sleep somewhere else."

He gave one of his chuckles. "A real goody-goody, you are!" He slapped his forehead. "Really a coward."

"You can think whatever you like," I said tiredly. I went out and stood in the passage. Appa's door had stayed open, I suspected that he might have heard our voices. I stood waiting until Shiva came out. Without looking at me standing there at the end of the passage, he went down the stairs. As I watched him enter the guest-room, I turned and noticed Raasamma standing near the kitchen door.

"God." I muttered. Going into my room, I shut the door and latched it. "Fool! Fool!" I cursed. Was I cursing Shiva, or myself? I didn't know. It felt like Amma telling me: "Don't go blundering into some mess." I felt an inexplicable rage. "I know all about it! I don't need anybody's advice!" I told myself. My heart was still thumping, my fingers trembling. I opened the medicine cupboard, gulped down a sedative, put off the light and lay down. Tears came, for some unknown reason – the tears that did not come when Shanbagam died. A real dope you were, Shanbagam. You deluded yourself. What Paavaayee said was quite true, my stomach *is* burning.

"Sleep, kannu! Kannu…sleep…" Shiva hissing into my ear. In between an uneven procession of women, approaching in scattered clusters, raising ululations, calling Mangamma by name, and shedding copious tears. An old woman lamenting –

. . . if I told you my woe
your bright golden face
will lose all its glow. . .

while African women weep, recalling everything they have lost. Weeping for themselves.

I opened my eyes to the morning. A dawn, the colour of ashes looked in at the window. I thought of how, in all innocence, Kunti recited a mantra, and how the Sun God suddenly stood before her. Again and again the same words. If she could have said "Abort it, doctor, as soon as you see it on the scan screen!"– – if only such a facility had been available to her — there wouldn't have been much to distinguish her story from the story of any woman in this town.

With a jerk I got out of bed. Today there was a lot of work to be done. Shanbagam's body had to be sent away. Not only had her relatives to be informed, Perumaal too had to be told, I decided. When I tell him, "Bleeding. She bled to death." I wanted to see if his face would change.

I wanted to leave for the clinic before Shiva got up. Had the events of last night brought Shiva closer to me, or had they driven him away? I was confused. "Goody-goody!" he had said, and hit himself on the head. Splashing water on my face and raising my head to look at myself in the bathroom mirror, even now my face reddens at the memory. "Fool!' I said to Shiva, fantasizing that he was right there in front of me. "You thought I would come to you as soon as you called me to bed. Exhausted, in mental anguish as I was, you tried to take advantage of me — what kind of man are you? You, who said you had accepted my conditions and agreed to come here, why didn't you respect my feelings of propriety?" As soon as the question surfaced in my mind, I forced it down again. I shouldn't attribute ulterior motives to his action. He didn't know Shanbagam had died. He thought he could exercise his right over the woman he was marrying, a man in the grip of a romantic passion — that was the state of mind in which he had turned up in my room.

This body is shameless, akka!"

Shanbagam's words were appropriate for Shiva, and for me, too.

Quickly I bathed and dressed. Raasamma had been standing at the kitchen door last night. What must she have thought! First of all, I must dispel her suspicions. If her opinion of me became diminished, the very basis of our relationship would be altered. 'Right' and 'wrong' had fixed boundaries about which she was absolutely clear in her mind. Besides, for a woman who had seen a number of Tamil movies, the salient features relating to female virtue were a matter of staunchly unshakable faith. That this concerned a couple who were going to get married was a consolation that would never occur to her. I could imagine her declaring: "Until the sacred marriage thread circles the neck, such a thing as marriage is far from certain!" She would say, "In how many movies has this happened? Right at the moment of tying the *taali*, a voice will suddenly announce, 'Stop!' And the marriage is stopped!"

What would Appa think if he came to know that Shiva had spent the night here in the house – the thought nagged at me. I looked into Appa's room. He was sleeping. I stood looking at him for a bit, and then went downstairs. Raasamma was boiling milk in the kitchen. "Can you give me some coffee," I said, "I have to go to the clinic."

"Here, it is," she said, pouring the coffee to cool it. "Is it some urgent case? You went out at two-thirty in the night didn't you?"

"Yes. You know that Shanbagam? She died," I said, dejectedly.

"Ah, di!" said Raasamma, wide-eyed. "Poor miserable thing! They said she fainted and fell down during yesterday's pujai."

Pushing away my empty tumbler, I said, "I'm going. If Appa wakes up, attend to him. If the guest – that ayya — asks, tell him I have left on some urgent work."

"That ayya has already left, at five-thirty," Raasamma said, with her head lowered.

I regarded her for a while, thoughtfully. Then in a low tone I said, "Raasamma, last night nothing happened. Nothing out-of-the-way."

At once she glanced up at me. The tension in her face relaxed perceptibly. Ashamed, I averted my face.

"You think I don't know you, `nga?" she exclaimed, brightly.

Again I said, reluctantly, "Don't tell Appa that he spent the night here."

"I won't tell, `nga." There was real friendliness in her tone. "I am also a woman, you know?" Then, as though to herself—"If anybody outside comes to know of course they will start talking," she said conspiratorially. "Even if it is only the future maapillai."

I didn't ask —who told you so? She would have replied —the whole town knows it. Indirectly reproaching me for not having told her myself.

"I have to go," I said, putting an end to the conversation.

I hurried to the clinic. By then Shanbagam's mother and brothers had arrived. Seeing me, the men covered their mouths with their towels. With an open-mouthed "O!" the mother began to weep out loud. I caught her shoulders. "I did everything I could, Muniamma! I couldn't save her," I said, in a defeated voice. "Her condition was very bad when she got here. What could I do?" She said nothing. Racked by sobs, she gestured to me as if saying, "Don't explain anything." Everybody had heard numours. The sons would have found out as well, I thought to myself. Taking the older of the brothers with me to hand over the body, I went inside. His face was grim as he silently paid the amount due to me. "We will bring a cart to take away the body," he said shortly. Shanbagam's death might have even been a relief for him, I thought. When he left the room, I heard loud talk at the gate. I looked out of the window.

Perumaal stood there. With arm upraised, Shanbagam's brother was about to strike him, when Perumaal gripped his arm and said in a loud voice, "All the while you could count on the money she was earning you sat around comfortably! You let her graze all over town like a cow let loose, and now you want to catch any man you can get and put the blame on him, eh? Thhoo! Worthless fellows! If you say anything, I'll break your teeth!" Before anything more disgraceful could happen, the spectators pulled them apart. Silence fell.

The younger brother brought a horse-cart. As the older one carried the corpse out and put it in the cart, Muniamma struck herself on the breast and wept. After they had all left, Perumaal approached me.

"What is the matter, Perumaal?" I was burning with outrage.

"Nothing, `nga. I came because I heard that again there was a case."

"Don't say 'again'!" I said angrily. "This is the first case. That, too, she came in a condition for which I could not have done anything. Do you know how she died? 'A case of natural death due to bleeding!'"

Inclining his head meekly, he heard me out. "All right, 'nga," he said and took himself off. It frustrated me that his expression revealed nothing. Again and again his wounding words came back to me – "*letting her graze all over town*". It was possible for me to question him and get him to admit his responsibility but what if he retorted, "She wanted it and came to me. Am I responsible for that?" I would have no answer to that. "I am in no way responsible for what happened afterwards either!" he would also say. "So, it came into the stomach? So what? That is woman's business! She has to manage it herself."

But surely Shanbagam's death must have affected him at least a little?

There was no emergency case at the clinic today. The woman who had delivered yesterday had no complications. She would be able to go home in a couple of days. I was in no mood to see any patients. Instructing Meenatchi to tell them all to come tomorrow, I left for the house.

Appa's managers were in his room, having some kind of earnest discussion with him. I flopped down on my bed without even changing my clothes.

"Why, are you tired, akka?" Raasamma asked, as she came in.

"A bad headache," I remarked, taking the coffee she had brought. "I stayed up almost the whole night but I could not save her."

"Disgraceful death it was, akka!" she said. "What could you do for her? She spoiled things herself."

"Raasamma, I have to sleep a little. Close the door behind you. What's that in your hand?"

"Oh... look at me! I almost forgot —there's a letter for you," she said, handing me an envelope.

Kamalini's handwriting. She must have written about her wedding. I'll read it later, I thought, and shut my eyes. I fell asleep out of sheer physical exhaustion. Raasamma woke me for lunch at noon, telling me Appa had eaten and gone to sleep. Since I had not had tiffin that morning, hunger pinched at my stomach.

As I rose after the meal, the telephone rang. Raasamma hurried to get it. Then, regarding me solemnly, she whispered, "Maapillai-ayya!"

As soon as I said, "Hello?" the question, "How are you, kannu?" created that same sensation of quivering deep down in my belly. The thought occurred to me that this was a chemical reaction. It and I – we had no connection with each other.

"I'm okay," I said, trying to sound matter-of-fact. "Are you angry?" he said, gently.

"Suppose I say yes. What will you do?"

"Every night I will come and pacify you!" He guffawed at his own witticism.

"Only if you're let inside, of course," I said, lightly. "When you come into this town, you'll get respect only if you follow the ways and customs of this town!"

"All right, I'll remember that," he said in a suddenly subdued tone. "It's only now, little by little, that I am beginning to understand the ways and customs of your town... and if you go on nodding and saying okay to everything, you'll be a dope."

"I don't understand what you are talking about," I retorted.

"It's *your* family matter, amma! Why should I say anything?" he queried, with a finicky air. Playing hard to get.

"Tell me," I insisted.

"Something that reached my ears – about your father. He's going in for adoption. To manage the company's affairs, they say. Also, to light the funeral pyre. That's what they say. But it sounds like nonsense!"

"Who said so?" My voice trembled. It was stuck in my throat.

"Several people are talking about it, what does it matter who said what?" His voice was indignant. "Can your father do such things without your knowing anything about them? It surprises me!"

"He will not do this. What you have heard is not true." But I did not believe my own words.

"I don't know." He sounded uncertain. "They say hereabouts that is the custom when there's no son `born from the belly', they call it."

"Even if it is the custom, I don't think Appa would do it." Eleven years ago Amma had said the very same words. I felt enfeebled by the memory.

"In that case, talking to your father and clarifying things is in your interest," he said.

It sounded like advice. It also sounded like a command.

Sixteen

"This is nothing that you need to concern yourself with, Shiva," I said, nettled. "So far I have managed on my own."

"Sorry, " Shiva said, quickly climbing down. "I don't want to interfere in your family matters. I just told you because I heard rumours. Forget it. How is your patient?" he said, changing the subject.

"She died last night."

He gave a low whistle. "Shit" he said, in English, as though cursing himself. "Sorry, Mano. Sorry. Please forget it."

"Forget what?"

"Everything. Tomorrow, or the day after tomorrow, I'll come and see you," he said, and hung up.

For some time I sat as though stunned. *"If you go on nodding your head and saying okay to everything, you'll be a dope."* Spoken by Shiva, in the guise of Amma, the words had stung. But now nothing hurt. Except for the news he had brought.

Your father is going in for adoption.

Without my knowledge? I who lived under the same roof? Could it be true?

Several people are talking about it.

Shiva had arrived in Salem just a few days ago. Had he really planted his feet so firmly there that "several people" could discuss such a subject with him? I thought it very surprising. Maybe somebody had put it into his head that "several people" were talking thus, somebody with the helpful thought that he should be told, since he was the "future maapillai".

The more I thought about this, the more I felt overwhelmed by an uncontrollable feeling of insult. It made me wild with Appa. If this were true, then it was not only I whom he had insulted, it was himself too.

Him? What can be wrong with HIM? Looks so fine he can be offered a seat and given in marriage.

The anger that had reverberated in Amma's voice had come from the same feeling of insult, I realized now. I had deluded myself that I had risen several levels above Amma's situation. That I had attained a great height. Yet, just two sentences had brought my house of cards tumbling down, without so much as a sound.

To manage the company affairs. Also, to light the funeral pyre. That's what they say.

I now understood that it was because he considered it unnecessary for me to know anything about the company's affairs that Appa had never kept me informed. And it was undeniable that I, too, had never shown any interest or eagerness in finding out about them. As though Appa were immortal or something! But to go in for adoption for such a reason? Wouldn't his managers and supervisors carry on as always? To snatch away my right, for whatever reason, was wicked! A crime against Dharma!

But how could I say this to a person who was still in a fragile state of health? How was I to make it clear to him that to push me to a point where I had to ask such questions was in itself a shamefully uncivilized thing?

Feeling defeated, I got up. Raasamma was sitting in front of the TV.

"They are showing 'Shiva Kavi'[4], 'kka," she said brightly.

"You watch. I am going upstairs." As I climbed up I saw that the goddess Parvati had miraculously appeared before Thyagaraja Bhagavathar, and was bestowing a boon: "From now on," she informed him, "you will be hailed as the Poet Who Never Spoke a Lie.'"

Without even thinking of looking in on Appa to see if he had woken up, I went towards my room.

"Akka!" I turned, hearing Maanikkam's voice. He stood in front of Appa's room as though he had been waiting for me to come upstairs. "Ayya has asked for you to come in."

All at once, I felt fear clawing at my abdomen. Forgetting all the thoughts that had just been heaving and rolling through my mind, I rushed in. Appa was in a state of extreme exhaustion. Swiftly reaching his side I clasped his hand and asked, "Did you call me? How do you feel?"

"Nothing special, amma," Appa said. "Since morning I hadn't seen you. So I asked for you. What is this, about that Shanbagam – she has died, I heard?"

In his eyes was such shock and incredulity that I was alarmed. "Did Maanikkam tell you? What a fool!" I remarked. Before I could upbraid him, Maanikkam quietly slipped away.

"Since you were not to be seen, I grilled him with questions and made him tell me. Don't go and scold him," Appa said. "I didn't expect Shanbagam to come to such an end, amma! And this is the very first time we have had a death in our nursing home, isn't that so?"

"Yes, appa," I said dejectedly. "I tried my utmost but I just couldn't save her. When I was not here, she got her pregnancy aborted by somebody or the other. It became septic."

"I can't believe it, amma. A very dignified woman! Who'd think she would do anything wrong?"

Like a whiplash came the rage. It felt as though all the dormant insults that I had suffered since the time I was born were being slapped awake.

"Why? Did you ask who was the man who was an accomplice in this wrong-doing? He wears a police uniform! Talks about law, talks about justice! Even now he must be prowling around in search of any woman foolish enough to have a smiling face! Nobody is able to question him about anything! Bring a witness, he says! It was only that stupid Shanbagam who had to suffer punishment! She actually died."

"I heard," Appa murmured. All of a sudden I had no desire to look Appa in the face. Wave after wave of indescribable fury came bursting out of me. There seemed to be no force capable of quelling me. The words emerged, exploding from my tongue:

"It is only the woman you'll all thrash, isn't it? It's only she who can be easily cheated, isn't that so? Do you need something? Then if you need it, it has a price, give it! Isn't that the way at every stage conditions are imposed on her, among our people? We want a male heir, they ask. If it is a girl, wipe it out, thayee! When each and every woman catches hold of my feet and begs me, how do you think I feel? As though the mother who gave me birth is herself begging me! When I see a female foetus on the scan screen, what do you think it reminds me of? My Amma, crying one evening, at the time when the lamps are lit. That is what it reminds me of. 'Adi, because you are a daughter, you aren't worth even a speck! Seems he needs a male as his heir, and so he is getting married a second time!' I remember how she cried! I get into a real fit, thinking will this child suffer the insult that I have suffered, and so I destroy it, and then sleep won't come, and I suffer more! I think maybe the woman who gave me birth may understand it, now that she is a ghost, that's the madness that gets hold of me, every full moon night, and every new moon night. When you said they are looking for a man to light Pandurangan's funeral pyre, I got angry for this same reason. When you repeat the same belief that illiterate people have, I realize that you have not yet changed! It makes me angry. Deep in my mind I realize that you are not satisfied, even if the whole world appreciates me and glorifies me. As though you are thinking:

Ayyo! I only have a daughter, she's not even fit to light my pyre!"

I stopped with a jerk, aghast at my folly in speaking thus. Appa sat regarding me steadily for a little while. Then he gave a gentle laugh. He could not laugh any more, though, because he started coughing. Tears spilt from his eyes. Agitatedly I rubbed his chest, and made him sip water.

"Sorry, 'pa," I said huskily. "Somehow the words slipped out." I felt miserable.

"Is that what your problem is?" said Appa. "You yourself should light my pyre. You alone? Apart from you, who else do I have?"

In an instant I was devastated. Pressing my face against Appa's chest I sobbed out, "Forgive me, Appa. I couldn't forget. Forgive all the old things."

Appa silently stroked my hair.

"I hear all sorts of things. So it...spilled out."

I sensed Appa suddenly becoming very aware... "What did you hear?" he said, slowly.

"That you are going to adopt someone," I said, raising myself.

Lines of thought snaked across Appa's face. "People will let loose some rumour or other, amma. What else do they say?"

"What else?"

Appa sighed. "Something bigger than that may reach your ears."

"What is it?" I asked, fearfully.

"I will tell you tomorrow. The situation will be a little more clear. Not today," he said tiredly.

"As you wish."

He looked worn out, in need of rest. But suddenly he said, "Doctor Shiva...You know him well, isn't that so?"

"Yes, Appa. Why?"

"Nothing... But could he have agreed to this marrige because of the value of our property?" It is a possibility that we should not set aside."

"I don't think he has such an idea. If it is like that, then I will not get married. I know how to take care of myself, 'pa."

Appa gave a small, sad smile. He stayed quiet for a long time. At last, with some effort, he said, "I hurt your mother's feelings once, out of some foolishness. Till today I regret that, amma. Not even a whiff of such trouble should ever blow in your direction – that's all I desire. It is not that the company affairs should not be told to you. Why should I burden you with all that, as well — that's what I thought."

Again tears sprang to my eyes. Appa had never spoken his mind openly to me like this before.

"Do I lack for anything, Appa? I'll be all right, don't worry."

"Somehow, I feel as if I have failed in my duty."

"Chhee chhee. Please don't talk," I said, tenderly chiding him. "I don't require your money or your property or anything. Even if you leave it to some orphanage, I'll be quite happy. What is important to me is the relationship between us."

Appa stared at me for a while. As though he didn't believe me. Then he shut his eyes and slowly said, "It is God I have to thank for this." Then, as though he had suddenly thought of something, he said, "Mano. Don't show your anger to the child in the womb, amma. Why do you want to spoil the chance of a girl like you being born?"

By the time I returned to my room an ineffable peace had entered my mind. I felt such a softening of the heart that I wanted to hum along with the song of Bhagavatar's that came floating up from below. Only then did my eyes alight on Kamalini's letter, lying unopened upon my table. I lay in bed and opened it unhurriedly.

"I have got married," she began. "Don't scold me for not sending you an invitation. Invitations were not even printed. It was a registered marriage. Lunch in a hotel for just ten of our close friends. I didn't even buy a new sari. Even though sharing a house with another person is a little strange for me, it is quite an experience.

"How is your father's health? I think he must have recovered well. It is not enough if you just have affection for your father. You have to come out with what is on your mind. Your estimation of him actually seems to me to be rather old-fashioned, an expression of a traditional way of thinking. You must try to change that."

Upturning the letter upon my chest, I closed my eyes. I felt abashed at how correctly Kamalini judged me. Despite remembering Amma, I had not freed myself from her fears, I had not been ready to forgive Appa. I ran my eyes again over the rest of Kamalini's letter. That was when I saw the lines:

"... a friend of mine came from Hyderabad. I asked him about your friend Shiva..."

In the evening when I had finished at the clinic and returned home, Raasamma told me that Appa's managers were sitting and talking with him in his room. I considered asking them about the problem that was troubling Appa. Within me was a prickling, a nagging question: What had Appa meant when he hinted: "Something bigger than that may reach your ears"?

I doubted that they would give me a proper answer. When Appa himself had told me that he would disclose it on the following day, there was really no need to find out from them, I thought to myself. Another warning thought held me back: since, contrary to what had been usual with him, Appa had now begun to confide in me, I must not be in too much of a hurry. Yet, I was tormented by the fear that any crisis situation in the company might have an adverse impact on him in this condition. I decided that I must make it very clear to him that more than his wealth and property and the comforts they brought, his health was what was important to me. As soon as they had left I went to see him. He was lying there with his eyes shut. Worry, or bodily pain, had etched deep lines on his face. I placed my hand on his forehead. He opened his eyes and gave me a faint smile.

"You look so tired — why not avoid discussing office matters for a few days?" I reproached him. "I am not going to allow these people in here again. Every time after they have left I can see you're much more tired than before."

Mutely Appa closed his eyes.

A little later he announced: "They will come tomorrow. I have told them not to come after that." His fatigue, and the sorrow in his expression churned my stomach. Stroking his forehead, I said in desperation, "Appa, I don't know what your problem is. Tell me tomorrow. There's no hurry. I'll manage it. I am educated. That's the best wealth anybody can ever have. That wealth is what I myself fought for so obstinately —do you remember the tantrums I had, Appa?" A soft smile spread over his lips.

"I remember very well," he said, without opening his eyes. "You were not the only one who had a tantrum. Your mother had one, too."

I sat there, dissolving in utter amazement. That Amma had played a part in my education was something I had never known.

"She was a woman of great foresight, amma. A prophetess! With all that, she had never stepped into a school."

The memory of Amma had brought a lingering smile to Appa's lips. He needs rest, I thought, and got up. But I stayed standing there, watching him sink into deep sleep.

When I did, finally, return to my room, it occurred to me that in the half-hour I had spent with him he had attained a kind of peace. And strangely, my own mind felt light, as though it had been divested of some great burden. For, from the day I had begun to comprehend things waves of restlessness had been buffetting me this way and that. Now it appeared that they had been quelled and calmed without any undue bustle. I felt as if I had acquired the maturity to endure all disappointments and sorrows, whatever they were, from now on. It seemed like a miracle. And as even Kamalini's letter effortlessly detached itself from my consciousness, sleep came peacefully.

I had a dream. Of Amma, who never had come to me in my dreams before. There she came, bearing herself along like a queen, with me holding her hand, and we were going to the weekly market in the village maidan, the Tuesday *sandai.* The ghee-sellers are clamouring, trying to tempt us. "Mustn't lose your head," she tells me, in confidence. "If you are vigilant, no fellow can cheat you." She smells them all, all the samples of ghee being held out to her, and walks on.

"Akka, akka, Mano Akka!"

A banging at the door. Maanikkam shouting…I wake up in a fright. Fear sweeps instantly over me as I hurry and open the door. Maanikkam is on the edge of panic.

"Ayya is not getting up, though I called him and called him. At one o'clock at night he asked for water, and drank a glassful."

As I took in what he was saying I ran to Appa. His face was serene, as though he was sleeping peacefully. The smile that had been on his lips last night when I left his room was still there. Like a maniac I took his pulse and searched for his heartbeat with my stethoscope. There still remained a faint warmth in his body. I broke into a sweat of fear.

"When did you last look in at Appa, Maanikkam?"

Already Maanikkam's eyes were full of tears.

"At one o'clock in the night, akka. At that time there was nothing wrong, he was quite all right. Then he went off to sleep,'kka. In the morning when I tried to see if he was awake, I got worried…"

I could not speak. It felt like a boulder had somehow climbed on top of my chest. Feeling as though my breath were about to stop, I gasped out, "Appa must have thought he was giving us all trouble. He has gone in his sleep, Maanikkam."

"Ayya!" Maanikkam moaned out loud. He began to weep great heaving sobs. I knew that Appa had been like a father to him. Many were the children he had, though he had not begotten them. I buried my face in his chest and sobbed. It was because he did not wish to live that he had died so quickly it seemed to me. Or maybe, having obtained answers to some of the questions that had tormented him, he had parted with life out of a feeling of relief. Now I became aware of new meanings to some of the things he had said to me yesterday. As though our conversation had been a short rehearsal for the actual event of death.

But what had happened to the thing he was about to tell me? Had he decided that there was no necessity for it? Or had he suddenly been in a hurry to die? I could not stand it. Tearing aside all my inhibitions, the tears burst out. Weeping herself, Raasamma tried to soothe me. It was Maanikkam who phoned the managers and gave them the news, and he informed me of their shock. He said that they had gone to an important court hearing, and would arrive at twelve. What did it matter who came, and when they came? It didn't matter to me at all. Appa's circle of friends and relatives was unimaginably large. It was Maanikkam who got down to the job of informing them all. Already people had started turning up. They kept on whispering amongst themselves, shutting up when they saw me, and then resuming their whispering.

While this was going on, Raasamma asked, "Akka, you have sent for maapillai-ayya, haven't you?"

"I don't even have his telephone number," I told her, and she gave me a strange look.

Thanikaachalam and Sambandham arrived at twelve o'clock, as they had said they would. Replying to somebody who asked the question, Thanikachalam announced:

"It was Ayya's wish that his daughter alone must light the funeral pyre. He has given it in writing."

When I held the torch tipped with a flaming ball of cotton cloth to Appa's body and set it on fire, although it was a deed never done by any woman in that town before me, it didn't feel like a great triumph. My dream came to mind —of myself, running with the flaming torch in my hand.

No woman should ever have such a dream again, I thought to myself.

Later that afternoon Thanikaachalam and Sambandham were waiting to talk to me.

"What happened to the court case?" I enquired.

"We lost it," a Thanika chalam replied.

"Tell me all about it in detail."

Appa had incurred unexpected losses in the share market. Taking advantage of this, his partner in the cotton mill had let him down badly. Although right had been on our side we had lost the case because of inadequate proof. "Except for some lands and this house, Ayya arranged to sell everything and settle the debt. This was the cause of his heart attack," said Sambandham.

I sat there in a state of shock. I understood that Appa hadn't wanted me to suffer from any of these anxieties. That was why he had kept his business affairs from me. That was his great mistake, I thought, grief-stricken. He could have set my mind at rest long ago with those words that he had spoken to me yesterday.

Shiva came in the evening. "What is this, you didn't inform me at all?" he said. "By chance a person in Salem asked me, 'Your father-in-law has passed away, aren't you going?'"

"I don't even have your telephone number, Shiva," I mumbled, with my head bowed. Then I looked up and said, "Whatever you heard the other day was wrong, Shiva. Appa did not adopt anybody."

"Yes. I came to know later on that that bit of news was incorrect."

He sat silent and subdued. After a pause, he cautiously began, "At such a time I should not start such a subject, I know. But I think it is good to know. As long as your father was alive, you didn't want to be separated from him, and for that reason you said I must come and stay here. Are you saying the same thing now also?"

I didn't speak, for some time. So that I could arrange the words properly, in my mind.

"I have to remain here, in this town."

"Why?"

"That is difficult to explain, Shiva. This is the place where there is work for me to do."

"But you can practise this profession anywhere, can't you?"

"'Work' is not the same as 'profession'. I have to make amends for some of the things I have done."

I didn't worry about whether he comprehended what I was saying. "Shiva, " I went on, "just because you gave your word, there is no need at for you to feel bound by it."

As though pondering over it, he sat there, with his head bowed. Then:

"I have to talk to you calmly later. It looks as though my practice will not strike roots in Salem."

Abruptly' he rose. "Don't think I've come to any decision. Things have not happened the way I thought. We'll talk about it later, calmly."

He came close and pressed my shoulder. "I understand your sorrow. Slowly, slowly it will heal."

Later. Calmly.

He would never talk about it again I knew. The dreams and illusions concerning him had been dispelled when I had read what Kamalini had written:

"In his field of medicine Shiva has become well-known as an expert. But he's also a person with an urge to make quick money.

There are reports that he has got involved in some shady dealings. It looks like it was just to set right those problems that he consented to marry you. Right now what he is most in need of is money."

The words had not particularly shocked me. Small things he said and did, some of the movements he made, even the most minute, the smallest things he did had been continuously sending me warning signals. As soon as he had discovered that Appa's business had collapsed he was drawing back. I felt ashamed that Appa's suspicions had been proved right. His sudden death was like a pall of smoke, it grieved me terribly. And yet there was a pervading sense of relief.

"There is one patient left, akka," said Meenatchi.

"Send her in," I said.

As though floating along in a dream, a woman came and stood before me. A bag-of-bones....She looked familiar.

"Aren't you an old patient — Ranjitham?"

"Yes, thayee. You saw a girl child in my womb and got rid of it, remember?"

I felt pain pierce me through. I hung my head and asked her, "What have you come for? Another pregnancy?"

"Yes, thayee," she said, her sunken cheeks wrinkling in a grin. "It is only three months. Take a look and tell me, thayee!"

I covered my face with my hands. Then I looked at her and smiled.

"From now on I won't do such things. I've taken a vow."

"Why, thayee?"

"Last full moon, during the pujai Mangamma's spirit came and said that from now onwards all the girl children who are born in this clinic are going to bring great prosperity to their parents' homes."

She stared in amazement. "Is that what it said?"

"Yes."

"Will my husband believe it?"

"Make him believe it! It's up to you."

She remained standing there, looking uncertain. I got up.

"It is all in your hands, just keep that in mind. Tomorrow if you have a girl, she'll become a doctor, like me!"

"Really? Mangamma says that?"

"Yes," I said, laughing and patting her shoulder.

As I came out, Meenatchi and the other women were getting ready for the full moon pujai.